Dragon Knights

Hidden
Dragons

BIANCA D'ARC

Copyright © 2015 Bianca D'Arc
Cover Art by Angela Waters

Copyright © 2015 Bianca D'Arc

All rights reserved.

ISBN: 1506199887
ISBN-13: 978-1506199887

DEDICATION

This one is for the fans who have been with me from the beginning. The first *Dragon Knights* book came out in 2006. It was the first book I ever had published and it started something that has become much more than I ever expected. It started a whole new career for me—a girl who'd already had four or five previous occupations.

I've made so many good friends through my writing. Other writers, and especially a few readers who have become valued friends.

Many thanks especially to Peggy McChesney for her continued support and friendship. Sometimes we all need a word of encouragement, and Peggy has been there to offer that modicum of sage advice and positive pep talk for me from time to time. It is greatly appreciated, my friend!

And, as always to my family. I think, no matter how old you are, if you had a good experience with your parents, you will always miss them when they're gone. I owe many, many thanks to my mother, who encouraged my career change back in 2005 and never doubted me—especially when I doubted myself.

CHAPTER ONE

Isabelle went where she always did when things in the village got too rough for her. She wept quietly by the falls, about a quarter mile down the river from the outer boundary of the small village of Halley's Well.

It was so hard being all alone in the world. Since her mother had died, there was no one to dry her tears or tell her she had value beyond two hands that could work as hard as any others. Only her mother had made her feel special. And loved. And her mother had never told her she was the next best thing to worthless. Her mother had never belittled her for the way she thought or the things she could do that were just a little out of the ordinary.

Now that mama was gone, there was no protection for her against the world's hateful ways. No buffer between her and the mean people in the village who didn't like her for whatever reason—or worse—feared her.

There were even whispers going around that she was a witch, and in this small border village, that could prove very dangerous indeed. Isabelle didn't quite fear for her life…yet. But the threat was there.

That's why normally, she did her best to remember to keep her head down and not draw attention to herself. She didn't want anyone thinking too long about her and her differences. Despite the fact that she and her mother had settled on the outskirts of the village more than ten winters ago, they were still considered outsiders. It wouldn't do to remind everyone in the village just how different she was from them.

Luckily, while her mother had been taller than most of the men in the village and light-haired, while everyone else had dark complexions, Isabelle was only a little above average height for a woman. Her skin was three shades lighter than the villagers, but her mama had always claimed that was because they had come from the colder regions where the sun didn't shine as much as down here, in Draconia.

Mama had never let it be known among the villagers that they were not native Draconians. That would have been going a step too far. But Isabelle was pretty sure at least some of the natives—the smarter ones—had guessed their origins were not of this land. What little Mama had told Isabelle about her ancestry was wreathed in mystery, but she knew for certain her papa had been a warrior of great renown in the snowy region she remembered only vaguely from her childhood.

Ever since papa's death, she and her mother had been on the move. They had traveled steadily southward until they came to the border with Draconia, and crossed into the land of dragons. Mama had felt safer here. Eventually, they found Halley's Well and settled on the outskirts of the village.

For the first few months, Mama had been nervous and watching almost constantly for the arrival of strangers in the village. But they had never come, and in time, Mama had relaxed her vigilance somewhat. They had lived here in relative peace for a long time before illness struck like a dagger, killing her mother and half the village in a fortnight.

There was nothing Isabelle could do but carry on. She had buried her beloved mother and lived a half-life filled with grief and sorrow for a long time. This lonely river bank had become her favorite place to cry, which she did a lot at first.

Nowadays, the weeping was more under control, but as

she had recovered from her shock at the loss of her mother, so had the village slowly recovered from the great loss it had also suffered. The people were back to their usual suspicion and distrust now, and Isabelle's life was getting harder to live every day.

She often contemplated leaving. She could go on the road as her mother had. But Mama was buried here and where could Isabelle go, really? She had no notion of what lay any farther than the heartiest villager could ride in a day. After that, the world was almost a complete mystery to her.

Oh, she had heard the usual stories of Castleton and the Lairs that were spaced all through the country. She had even seen a dragon or two fly over from time to time as they patrolled the border. But all those stories seemed like fairytales to a girl who hadn't known anything but small village life and traveling through nearly deserted country. The idea of a city—where many, many people lived together in great stone houses and even castles—was hard to imagine.

Life was just so unfair. If Mama were here, she would have known what to do. Mama was always so decisive and full of good advice. She also gave great hugs, and she was the one person in the entire world that Isabelle knew loved her, with all her faults and foibles. Mama loved her just the way she was. Nobody else had ever cared for her—with the exception of Papa, perhaps, though he had died so long ago, it was hard to remember him at all.

"What makes you weep so, mistress?" A gentle, deep voice shocked Isabelle out of her misery.

Sniffling and wiping her eyes with sharp movements, she spun to find a man watching her. Not just a man. A knight, if the dragon standing behind him was anything to go by.

Sweet Mother of All! There was a dragon standing not ten yards from her and she hadn't heard a whisper of his approach.

Isabelle bowed her head in respect. "I'm sorry, Sir. I will leave you to refresh yourself." For what other reason would a dragon and knight come to ground but to take a break from

3

their journey and perhaps drink from the river?

She made to move past him, but the knight reached out and took her hand, making her pause. She looked up at him and found only kindness in his eyes. Beautiful blue eyes so very unlike the muddy brown of the villagers' condemning, dark gazes.

"Please stay, milady. We were about to enjoy our evening meal before we continue on night patrol. It's always easier to eat while there is still daylight to see by." His eyes crinkled at the corners when he smiled. "It would be nice to have someone to talk to other than Sir Growls-a-lot over there."

The dragon snorted and little tendrils of smoke wafted up from his nostrils as if he was amused. Isabelle stared at the dragon. He was amazing in every way. His scales sparkled in a lovely shade of dark greenish mixed with bronze that shimmered as he moved.

But dragons usually patrolled in pairs—or so the stories said. Isabelle looked around, wondering if another dragon lurked in the shadows on the other side of the small clearing.

"Surely you can converse with your partner?" she asked uncertainly, not sure if she should stay, but tempted beyond all reason to do whatever the handsome knight asked of her.

The knight laughed at her statement and let go of her hand. "Bear? That tree over there talks more than Sir Bernard the Quiet." Even the dragon chuckled again at this statement. "Please, milady, spare me another silent meal with my grumpy fighting partner. We have fruit bread and even some sweets to share, right Growly?" He looked back at the dragon, who bounced his head up and down as if he were answering his knight's question.

Isabelle was enchanted. She had never been so close to a dragon—or a knight, for that matter. She probably shouldn't, but she decided to stay.

"Why do you call him that?" Isabelle asked, blurting out the question before she could stop herself.

"Because he can't pronounce my real name," came an amused, dry, rumbly voice in her mind.

It felt warm to hear it. Comforting in a way she hadn't felt since Mama had died. Only her mother had been able to speak mind-to-mind with Isabelle in all her life, and Mama's voice was light and musical, very unlike the earthy rumble of the dragon.

She looked into the dragon's eyes, using the skill she hadn't practiced since her mother's death.

"Forgive me, sir. I didn't know dragons communicated in this way. I have never met one of your kind before."

The dragon's head reared back as if in surprise, but he quickly recovered, zooming in to stare at her intently with his crystalline, hazel-green eyes. He blinked at her, looking her over intensely, but she didn't mind his perusal. He seemed nice. So unlike the villagers who stared at her in hatred or fear. This dragon seemed intrigued, and almost...hopeful?

That couldn't be right, but then again, Isabelle had never talked with a dragon before.

"You can hear me?" the dragon seemed to want to confirm what had just happened.

Isabelle gathered her courage and smiled at the dragon. *"I can, sir. And I am honored to meet you, though I do not know your name."*

"Growloranth," came the stunned reply in her mind.

She made her shaky bow again. *"I am Isabelle."*

"She can hear me," Growloranth spoke directly into his knight's mind, shocking him.

"Are you sure?" Robert was amazed the small woman they had come upon in such a heartbreaking scene had hidden depths. Was this some kind of trick?

"Not only does she hear, but she speaks as if she has been doing it all her life." The dragon was duly impressed and sounded just as surprised as Robert was. *"Her name is Isabelle."*

"Isabelle?" Robert repeated out loud, and the woman turned. Her shy smile made him want to reassure her, but of what, he wasn't sure.

"Yes, forgive me again, sir. My name is Isabelle, as I just

told your partner, Sir Growloranth."

She gave Robert the same little bow she had given the dragon and Robert was impressed by her manners. Most border folk in the small villages like the one they had just flown over were either afraid or overly obsequious when they met knights and dragons.

This young woman had a confident interest that was as refreshing as it was attractive. Everything about her was pretty, from the glint in her green eyes to her pale skin and long, golden blonde hair. She didn't look like most border folk, who were usually dark-skinned and dark-haired. She had a bit of fey grace about her that made her stand out.

"No, I'm afraid you must forgive me, milady," Robert finally said, aware that he had been staring at her a little too long. "It is a rare thing to find someone who can speak with dragons. How in the world did you learn such a skill, living out here on the border?"

"My mother could speak in that way, mind-to-mind. She taught me. Since her death, I have spoken to no one else. It is...nice...to be able to use the ability again without fear," she admitted in a quiet voice.

"What do you fear?" Growloranth was instantly on guard, ready to defend her, it seemed.

"The villagers have never been very accepting of my differences. Even though we came here when I was young, we have always been considered outsiders. Now that Mama is gone, I've felt very alone, which is why I come down to the river..." she trailed off, looking at the spot where they had found her, crying.

"Your mother died?" Robert asked gently.

She nodded. "In the sickness that took half the town two years ago. It was very sudden."

"And you have been alone since? Have you no mate or younglings?" Growloranth asked quickly.

"No, sir," she answered in a quiet voice—out loud so Robert could also hear. "I have no mate or children. I live simply and work in the fields with the other villagers. I also tend the beasts when they are injured. For my work, I am given a small share of the community harvest. That, and my own small garden, is how I've survived these past years since Mama died."

The dragon looked at Robert, the censure in his eyes for the villagers clear. Robert knew Growloranth felt as strongly about injustice as he did. While they didn't have all the facts about this odd young woman yet, the picture they were starting to get didn't look good.

"She should be in the Lair," Growloranth sent to Robert privately. *"Women who can speak with my kind are rare enough. I am certain we could find a place for her in the Border Lair. And our folk would treat her well. Many of the knights would try to court her. She would not be alone for long. In fact, why don't you try your hand, Robert? I'd like to claim my mate sooner rather than later and you know I cannot do that until you and Bear find a mate to share. Lady Isabelle might be the one."*

Robert had already started thinking along those lines, but it wasn't just up to him. While the two dragons already knew they were mates, they were prohibited from actually mating until their knight partners had a wife.

The sad fact was, if the dragons engaged in a mating flight, linked so closely to their knights as they were, the knights would need to be able to express that same bond of love, lust and ecstasy with their mate. Being bonded to a dragon meant sharing a mate, since only men were chosen as fighting partners by dragons and once chosen, they spent their lives bonded to their dragon. Only death could break the bond and while the dragon's magic imparted an extended lifespan to most knights, the dragon would live on for many centuries after their knight had left this world.

Most often, the dragons of lost knights would go into a period of mourning for their departed bondmate. They would seek solitude high up in the mountains, living a simpler life for a decade or more. When they were ready, they would return to one of the Lairs and begin the search for a new knight to share their exceedingly long lives with, in defense of their shared homeland.

Any male who could hear a dragon speak in his mind, and was inclined to the life of a warrior, was eligible for a dragon to choose. The dragons had a way of seeing to the heart of a person, and once chosen, a partnership was for life, so they were very careful of their choices. Only the most noble and brave of men were chosen to fight alongside a dragon—and only those with the talent for speaking mind-to-mind.

Women with the skill were even rarer. Very few could hear or speak to dragonkind, and most were afraid. It was not easy to live with a dragon in the family—or two—which is how Lair families were formed. But certain special women made families with their knights and the dragons. Still, a mating in the Lair was a rare thing and something to celebrate.

If Isabelle could be a mate to Robert and Bear, it would be something incredibly special. And if not them, perhaps she would be a match for another pair of knights in the Lair. Her ability to speak with dragons, and her lack of fear of them, counted much in her favor.

"I'm with you, friend," Robert sent to Growloranth privately, knowing he had been silent too long. Again. "Milady, would you share the meal with us? And then, after, we will see you safely home."

"I don't want to impose," she said, biting her lip in the most innocent, enticing way.

"It is no imposition. We have plenty of food to share and unless I am much mistaken, our partners approach with some fresh meat. There will be enough for all five of us, and then some. Please stay."

She was about to answer when Tildeth and Bear stepped into the clearing…and Isabelle was entranced. Robert had to smile. Tildeth often had that effect on people. She was the most delightful shade of pale crystal blue. Together, she and Growloranth were a sight to behold. Light and dark. Bright day and shadowy night.

"Lady Isabelle," Growloranth said into the minds of all those present, *"please allow me to introduce my mate, Lady Tildeth."*

The stunning blue dragon walked up to stand beside Growloranth and rubbed her neck scales along his in greeting, while eyeing Isabelle. Bowing low, Isabelle returned the greeting mind-to-mind, making Tildeth blink.

"Lady Tildeth, it is my honor to meet you. And may I say, you are lovely." Robert could hear the genuine awe in Isabelle's tone as she broadcast her delicate voice for all those with the ability to hear.

Tildeth preened. She wasn't a vain dragon, though she had every right to be. She was one of the most graceful, well-formed female dragons of her generation. And her coloration was rare. She matched the sky almost perfectly, and was the next best thing to invisible during the day.

And her mate, Growloranth, was the exact color of a twilight forest. Between the two, they made a great team for stealth maneuvers.

"Thank you, Isabelle. It has been a long time since I spoke with one of your kind," Tildeth surprised them all by saying. Including, it seemed, Isabelle.

"Sorry. My kind?" Isabelle's head tilted in puzzlement.

"You may not look it, and it's probably dilute, but you have the blood of the Fair Folk in you, do you not?" Tildeth too, tilted her great head as if in question.

Understanding and a bit of shock dawned over Isabelle's features. "My mother was fair in complexion and face, but she never really spoke of her origins."

"It would make sense, though," Growloranth added. *"There is a flavor of magic about you that is completely benign, yet unfamiliar to me. I have never met a Fair One."*

"Trust me, the flavor of her magic is of the Fair Folk. I knew a few of them in my youth," Tildeth said. *"Can you not hear the musical note in her voice? The fey have the most musical of all voices."*

"Mama used to sing to me," Isabelle said softly, as if remembering, and her eyes took on a sad, faraway look.

Silence reigned in the clearing for a moment, the only sound that of the rushing water behind them. Bear chose that moment to step forward.

"I am Sir Bernard," he pronounced, his voice gruff, but a welcome distraction from the serious turn of their conversation. He offered his hand in greeting and Isabelle took it, allowing him to raise her small hand to his lips for a tender salute.

Robert cursed himself for not doing the same sooner. As it was, Bear had already touched the woman—even kissed her hand—and Robert had done nothing more than talk her ears off. He wasn't going to get anywhere in figuring out if she was their mate this way.

Sir Bernard—known as Bear to his friends—marveled at the beauty his partner had somehow found in the woods. Her skin was soft, even if she did have hands roughened from hard work. That was no sin. In fact, it showed just how much this gentle woman did to make her way in the world. He could not find fault with that. Not in the least.

Bernard might be gruff on the outside, but he had been raised in a family that respected hard work and honesty above all else. He had partnered with one of the loveliest dragons of their time and many had thought it a mismatch when Tildeth chose him, but Bear knew the truth. Tilly chose him for what was on the inside. Although pretty to look at, she saw straight to the heart of him, as he saw beneath her pretty shell to the heart of the warrioress that lay beneath her sky blue hide.

They were perfect for each other. The only thing that would make their partnership complete was if Bear could find a mate. And any mate Bear found would be shared with Robert because Tildeth and Growloranth were mates of long standing. Each had partnered at least one knight before Robert and Bear. They had lived for many centuries already and had two fully grown children. They had not been able to be together as mates since choosing Robert and Bear.

It hurt Bear to know that his single status kept his fighting partner from her mate. He would do just about anything for Tilly. She was part of him—bonded on a soul-deep level. But the mate bond could not be forced. Not just any woman would do. The woman that bonded with them and completed their family unit had to be just right. Destined for them by the Mother of All Herself.

"Do you think she could be the one?" Tilly asked Bear privately. *"Growloranth thinks she might be."* Bear noted the eager tone in his fighting partner's voice. He couldn't help but feel a bit of eagerness himself.

"I can't be sure yet. It is too soon. But I will say that she is lovely. I wouldn't mind spending the rest of my days with a creature as beautiful as Isabelle," Bear answered Tilly honestly. *"But outward appearances—as you well know—are not enough to base something so important on. We need to get to know her."*

"We need to get her to come back to the Lair with us," Tilly replied.

"I agree. Let me work on it. We will make this happen. I promise you."

"Nice to meet you, Sir Bernard," Isabelle replied to his kiss on her hand.

Reluctantly, he let her go and tried to smile. He had to be charming, which was difficult for a homely fellow like himself.

"Please, call me Bear," he offered, pleasure streaking through him when she smiled.

"Do people call you that because you're as big as a bear?" He liked the teasing, playful tone in her voice.

"That, and he usually growls like one," Robert put in. "And don't get me started on his snoring. We share a suite in the Lair and I can hear him all the way in my bedchamber, on the other side of the sand pit."

"That's a lie," Bear defended himself, even as he chuckled, used to Robert's easy manner. The Mother of All had given him a good match in the fun loving, mischievous knight. They might look like opposites, but they complemented each other.

Bear helped Robert focus and Robert helped Bear see the humor in life. They had become good friends—more like brothers—since being chosen by Tildeth and Growloranth a dozen years ago.

"So you two live together?" Isabelle asked, looking from Bear to Robert and back.

"All four of us share quarters, in fact," Tilly put in, craning her neck downward as her mate, Growloranth, removed the buck she had taken down from where Bear had put it over her back.

Growloranth moved away with his prize, using his sharp talons to skin and cut up the meat that the humans would eat. Bear watched Isabelle, who watched the dragons with rapt attention. When Growloranth shot a pinpoint of flame at his own forelimb, she jumped back a little, right into Bear. He put out his hands to steady her, caressing her shoulders.

"It's okay. He's cooking our dinner. See?" Bear whispered near her ear. He nodded toward Robert, sending a private message into his partner's mind. *"Go get the meat from your dragon. She's trembling. We have to prove our dragon friends are not dangerous to her."*

"Don't think I'm not taking note of how many times you've managed to put your hands on her," Robert growled back into Bear's mind, but he went anyway.

Robert collected the three steaks Growloranth had speared on one talon, using an old dragon scale as a platter. They kept a few of the dragons' shed scales with them for just such instances. The scales were incredibly strong and impervious to just about anything. They also didn't transfer heat. The steaks were sizzling on top of the scale when Robert brought them back to where Isabelle stood with Bear.

"I hope you like your venison well done," Robert said, grinning as he presented the makeshift platter for Isabelle's inspection.

"That's amazing. Thank you, Sir Growloranth," she said, turning to look at the dragons. They stood closer to the river, side by side. Bear knew they would share the rest of the deer as a snack. When they were done, there would be little left for the forest scavengers.

"You are very welcome, Lady Isabelle," Growloranth replied,

preening a little.

"Come, let's sit and eat," Bear invited, escorting her to the flat rocks by the small waterfall.

"She was sitting here, crying, when we found her," Robert imparted directly to Bear's mind, filling him in on what he'd missed while he and Tilly were hunting.

Robert also brought the bag of sweets and other provisions with him, and they set up an impromptu picnic on a large, flat boulder that peered out over the water's edge. It had been Robert's turn to make camp while Tilly and Bear hunted. The dragons enjoyed a good hunt, as did the knights, so they took it in turns to provide meat for the proverbial table while they were on extended patrols or special missions.

This time, it was the latter. Bear and his nearly invisible-in-daylight dragon would be flying forays over the border with Skithdron, doing reconnaissance. They were particularly interested in troop movements or, even worse, skith sightings along the border with Draconia. Not too long ago, the crazed king of Skithdron had tried to herd an army of the vile, venomous monsters over the border as a first wave of attack on the people of Draconia.

Dragons were the only real threat to the giant, snake-like skiths. Given enough concentrated flame, skiths could be turned to ash. And only dragons had that kind of firepower.

Skiths could spit their highly acidic venom for twenty feet or more. Only dragons had nearly-impenetrable scales that could withstand the acid long enough to fight the snake-like creatures. Many dragons and knights had been injured in battles on this border in recent years, and it was prudent to keep a close watch on the enemy forces positioned just over the rocky division between the two lands.

Tilly and Bear had been sent to the Border Lair for just that purpose. When it came to daylight flying, nobody was better suited to stealth with Tilly's almost reflective, sky blue hide. Bear wore specially-made light-colored leathers on their secret flights and took careful notes of whatever they saw.

Oddly enough, Growloranth and Robert were well suited

to another kind of stealth. They could blend in with almost any forest. Growloranth's bronze-green hue adapted really well to the dark part of a loamy forest. He also was almost as good as the royal black dragons at night flying.

"Do you live in the village we flew over, just to the west?" Robert asked Isabelle as they all settled on the large boulder and began to eat.

"Halley's Well. That's the name of the village," she answered as she accepted the smaller dragon scale upon which Bear had placed a portion of the meat and some of the other items they had with them. "I live on the outskirts, in the old healer's hut. Mama and I fixed it up as best we could since nobody else was using it. It's not far from here, through the woods. I come up here every day to fetch water."

"But isn't the village named for a well?" Bear asked, perplexed. If there was truly a well in Halley's Well, then why did Isabelle have to fetch water from the river?

"It is, but the villagers can be...difficult sometimes," she admitted. "Ever since Mama died, it's just easier to stay away from them when I can. I keep to myself for the most part."

"That doesn't sound very neighborly," Robert observed. Bear knew his partner was just as angry as he was about the way Isabelle seemed to have been treated by the villagers. They would have to investigate. There was no way around it.

"They are an...insular folk. They don't like outsiders and they never really accepted Mama and me. It's okay. I manage." She shrugged quietly and went about eating the meal they had provided.

The poor mite looked like she hadn't had a truly good meal in a long time. She savored every bite and seemed especially enraptured by the sweets. Bear unobtrusively put another portion of the sweet breads—his own portion, though he was careful to be sure she didn't realize it—on her dragon scale plate. She tried to demur, but he politely insisted and she smiled in thanks.

Her smile could light a room, he decided, stunned for a moment by the way her eyes seemed to glow with happiness at his small kindness. They talked of the river and how it was high for this time of year. They talked of the weather and of the wildlife in the area. Slowly, Bear came to realize that his canny partner was probing for just the sort of information they had been assigned to discover, among other things.

Bear suddenly realized that they could kill two birds with one stone. They could use Isabelle's knowledge of the surrounding area to their advantage, if she was willing. And by doing so, they could stay close to her for a few days.

"Are you thinking what I'm thinking?" Bear sent to Robert privately.

"If you're thinking we're going to camp near Isabelle's house, I'm way ahead of you, partner," came the dry reply.

"Milady Isabelle," Robert began, broaching the subject delicately. It wouldn't do to scare her off. "We have been dispatched from the Border Lair to do an in-depth survey of these lands. It was our intention to camp in the area for a few days and make our study, but we've never been here before and we could benefit from your knowledge. Would you be willing to aid us in our mission?"

Oh, that was very cleverly worded. Bear was glad yet again that he had been partnered with a knight who had a gift for oratory. Bear himself would have made a hash of it, he was sure, which was why he mostly kept quiet.

"I'm not sure what help I can be, but I am willing to assist if I can," she answered thoughtfully.

"There would be payment for your services. And we would not expect anything but that you share your knowledge of the area with us," Robert was sure to point out. "We can do surveys from the air—and of course, we will—but the trees often obscure what lies beneath. For that reason, Growloranth and I will be scouting on the ground each day while Bear and Tildeth take to the sky. Would you be willing to act as our guide on the ground? That is, if it doesn't interfere with your own work too much."

Bear was jealous as hell that Robert would get her all to himself all day while Bear and Tilly scouted in the air over the border, but it couldn't be helped. Bear trusted Robert to keep her safe and while it wasn't necessarily their mission to scout this side of the border, it wouldn't hurt.

Nobody from the Lair had been this far north in a very long time. Rumors of enemy infiltration of border towns were flying lately, and this was as good a place to start their reconnaissance as any. In fact, from what Isabelle had already revealed of the villagers' suspiciously bad attitudes, it was perhaps a very good place to begin.

"The harvest is in and my preparations for winter, such as they are, have been mostly completed," Isabelle said slowly. "I believe I could help you for a few hours each day. And…I'm not sure if you're interested…but I do have a barn of sorts where you all could camp out under a roof at least. It looks like it might rain before the dawn and I hate to think of you all suffering in the cold and wet out here in the woods."

Robert smiled broadly and shot Bear a triumphant look. "That sounds like a grand idea, milady. Thank you for your generosity."

CHAPTER TWO

Robert and Bear, plus the dragons, followed Isabelle to her home on the edge of the woods. Her small dwelling was situated on a rise above the rest of the village. It was a good vantage point to see anyone coming up the path, and gave a view of most of the village.

It was dark by the time they got to her place, and they could see the little dots of flame in the distance that marked the lights of people's homes. There weren't all that many. It was a very small village. But it was telling that they all clustered their houses together while Isabelle was sentenced to live up here on the edge of the wood, without the little protection afforded by clustering together with the rest of the inhabitants of the area.

Robert didn't like that at all. To him it was like the villagers just left her out here to fend for herself. What kind of people did that to a young woman who had lost her mother?

She showed them to the barn, located to the right of the house. The home itself was run-down, but the barn was even worse. Robert knew he would be making some repairs as soon as he was able. For now, at least, the place had a roof and enough space for the dragons and knights to shelter from the rain. It would do for the night. After all, they had intended to camp anyway. The roof and dry floor would be nice, since there was little doubt, as the night deepened, that it was going to rain by morning.

"There is firewood for the old forge. Before the healer lived here, it was a smithy, though the lighter equipment was taken away long ago. The forge remains and can be used for a fire, if you wish," Isabelle explained, showing them around. "I also have an oil lamp you can use for light." She reached up to take the lamp down from a peg. It was of simple design and only had a small amount of oil left in its base. Robert took it from her with a smile, though inside he noted the sparse way she lived and the lack of proper supplies in the barn. "Will you be warm enough?" She seemed to worry over how to provide for them.

"We will be fine, mistress," Robert reassured her. "Our companions provide plenty of heat, and we have supplies of our own. We had intended to camp all along, so we came prepared. Do not fret about us. We'll be all right. In fact, we'll be far more comfortable here than we would have been out in the forest with rain coming. Now, you go inside and take care of yourself."

She seemed to hesitate, but Bear, bless him, stepped forward. "Is there anything we can do for you before we all seek our rest?" Bear was gruff at the best of times, but he didn't seem to scare Isabelle, which was a very good sign.

"Oh, no. I am fine. Thank you, Sir Bernard." She looked at them all, the dragons standing behind their knights, every eye on Isabelle. "Good rest, then. I will see you all in the morning." She blushed, curtsied and then hurried away.

The knights watched her until she was safely inside and a lamp was lit. Robert followed her progress through the small house through the fabric-draped windows. The curtains were thin and allowed him to see the movement of her lamp through the building until finally, she seemed to settle in one place.

He wondered if she was sitting by a fire, or maybe lying in her bed. That thought led to much naughtier thoughts of her lying in *his* bed. Preferably naked.

"Are you going to help set up or stand their dreaming all night?" Bear asked, shouldering past Robert with a pack in his hands.

"Sorry." Robert shook his head to try and clear it. They had work to do.

As the lights in the village went out one by one, Robert and Bear crept down into the town, beginning their evaluation of the people who lived there. The dragons were up in Isabelle's barn, just a mental shout away if their knights ran into trouble, but this job was just a little too small in scale for their large bodies.

Robert and Bear were used to skulking around in the darkness. They examined the layout of the village, confirming most of what they'd seen from the air and learning new facets that could not be seen from above. For one thing, the largest home in the village was more or less hidden under trees, keeping it invisible from dragon overflights.

And it was a really big home. Incongruous given the general poverty of the homes around it. Robert was instantly suspicious. Hidden from view, the big house in a comparatively unfriendly village was something quite out of the ordinary.

"I think that place bears further scrutiny," Bear said into Robert's mind.

"Without doubt, my friend. Shall we check it out?"

They spent the next two hours listening at every window they could access and peering in wherever it was possible to do so without being seen. They also took a brief inventory of the outbuildings. There were three small sheds behind the main house in addition to a large barn that housed quite a bit of livestock including a number of horses that didn't look like any farm horse either of the knights had ever seen.

The rest of what they learned was equally as troubling. Silently, they agreed to halt their activities for the evening, heading back to Isabelle's barn as covertly as they had left it hours before.

The dragons were waiting when they arrived back at the warm barn. Luckily, the rain had held off for the most part. Only a light drizzle had dampened the mens' dark garments and the heat from their dragon friends soon had them dry and warm once more.

"Do you think this village is the one?" Tilly asked as they settled in for the night.

They were using a small camp lantern they had brought with them for light. There was no need of a fire, since the dragons would keep everything toasty warm just by their presence.

"I'm afraid so. Whoever lives in that big house is definitely a traitor," Robert said. "Those horses are war-trained. Not a one of them has ever seen a plow. What does a farmer have need of a war horse, much less a dozen of them? And where would he get such a beast this far from any training grounds?"

"So it really is this easy? The second town we look at is the one we want?" Growloranth asked the question they were all thinking.

"Well, in all fairness, we were only given five towns to check," Robert pointed out. "And we still will need to check the other three after we finish here. However, I think we've found what we were looking for, and we're going to have to act on it."

"But what about Isabelle?" Bear asked, clearly concerned.

"Aye." Robert shook his head. "We're going to have to sort things out for her before anything happens here. Otherwise she could be directly in the path of danger. For now, I think we should just stick close to her."

"You'll get no argument from me. She seems in need of our help, even if we can't ultimately convince her to come with us to the Lair. We can probably convince her to let us use her barn for the next few days while we continue our mission," Robert said, looking around at the dilapidated structure.

"Do you think she knows what's going on in the village?"

Bear asked the tough question that was hovering in all of their minds.

"I sincerely hope not," Robert said with intense feeling. "I want to believe the best of her, but if she knew about this and didn't tell us…"

"She could just be protecting herself," Tilly offered. *"After all, she believes she still must live here after we fly away. She has to get along with these people. Her life here is tenuous enough as it is, from all appearances."*

"Nevertheless," Growloranth interjected, *"while you are scouting tomorrow, I will keep an eye on our hostess. Robert is too enamored of her already to be objective."*

Robert wanted to argue with his dragon partner's assessment of his state of mind, but he couldn't. Growloranth was right. He wanted to believe the best of Isabelle and wasn't very objective when it came to anything about her. It had been a very long time since a woman affected him so strongly.

"While you're out scouting, I can stick around here and try to make things a little more comfortable—and sturdy—for her, while keeping an eye on the village," Robert added. "Growloranth can watch her. I'll watch the village, while I add some bracing to this barn's roof. Between the two of us, perhaps we'll come up with something useful."

"Sounds like a good plan to me," Bear replied.

They fell asleep shortly after the conversation drifted to a natural conclusion. The dragons kept watch. Nothing could sneak up on them with a dragon dozing nearby.

Nothing happened for the rest of the night as the rain poured down in earnest. It was a quick moving storm that was gone by the time dawn broke, waking Robert and Bear.

After what they had observed the night before, they were eager to get moving. Bear and Tilly took off shortly after dawn, on their planned scouting mission. They were going to fly over the border with Skithdron, to look for any telltale troop movements that might indicate an imminent attack.

That left Robert and Growloranth to work on watching

the village. They would start by shoring up the barn that looked like it might fall down at any moment. It was a rather oblique method of surveillance—watching from afar while accomplishing something else—but it was what was called for in this particular situation. Plus, Robert really wanted to help Isabelle. He could repair her barn for her, which gave him an excuse to hang around, but it also meant that he, Bear and their dragon partners would have a sturdier place to sleep while they were here.

In a way, it was very useful that Isabelle's home was so far out on the very edge of the forest. There was a clear approach to her place—a path that wound up from the village—that would make it easy to see if anyone was heading this way long before Growloranth could be spotted against the leafy backdrop of the forest.

Even so, the dragon would hang back, staying mostly to the cover of the trees while Robert stayed closer to the house and barn. Robert found an ax by the woodpile behind the house and took it out to the nearby woods to find a few small trees he could cut down that would work for shoring up the old timbers of the barn.

By the time Isabelle had come out of the house, an hour after dawn, Robert had already made good progress on fixing up the barn. She seemed surprised to see what he'd done.

"You've been busy," she observed, walking up to him as he propped the timber he had cut under the sagging roof. Growloranth was helping, his strength making the otherwise difficult task an easy fix.

"It is the least we can do since you opened your home to us," Growloranth answered before Robert could speak.

She didn't seem to know what to say to that, so Robert stepped in, dusting his hands off as he moved closer. He smiled, hoping to put her more at ease.

"Did you sleep well, mistress?" Robert asked conversationally.

"Very well, thank you. And you?" Back on firmer ground with the exchanges of polite conversation, she seemed more at ease.

Robert grinned. "Much better than if we had camped the way we originally planned. It poured down rain in the hours before dawn."

"Is that what woke you so early?" She moved into the barn, looking around at the progress he had made in the last hour. "You've been *very* busy."

"We are early risers in the Lair, for the most part. Working with Tilly, we are often assigned day shifts because of her color."

Had he said too much? Robert couldn't bring himself to suspect Isabelle of knowing about the treason in the village...and yet...he had to keep an open mind. More than just his mission depended on it.

"It is easy to see why she is best suited to daytime work. But what of your dragon partner? Doesn't he stand out against the blue, daytime sky as much as his lady blends?" she asked, nothing but curiosity in her tone that he couldn't fault, even if her questions were almost too astute.

"I do," Growloranth answered for himself, coming out of the darkness at the rear of the barn, where he'd been doing his best to blend into the shadows. Isabelle jumped a little. and one small hand went to her chest. *"Apologies if I frightened you, mistress. Actions sometimes speak louder than words, so I thought it prudent to show you one of my talents. I blend in very well with forests and dark spots."*

"So you do, Sir Growloranth," she agreed, smiling a bit at the dragon's theatrics. "You do that very well indeed." She chuckled, the sound musical and light, then turned back to Robert. "I came out to see if I could offer you breakfast, but I see I am too late for Sir Bernard. Did he and Lady Tildeth go somewhere, or will they be back in time to eat with us?"

"As I think we mentioned yesterday, we were sent here to do a survey of the land in these parts. That is Bear's specialty. He and I agreed he would start work while I did a few repairs to repay you for your kindness in letting us sleep here last night," Robert stated. Now he had to find a way to get her to let them stay longer. Chatting over breakfast might just be useful in that regard. "I haven't eaten yet, if the offer of breakfast is still open," he volunteered.

"It is," she agreed, smiling. "It is only oat mash, but it is hot and filling."

"It sounds perfect. With the chill in the air, it's good to have hot cereal of a morning," he said heartily, wiping his hands as he followed her toward the house.

When he stepped inside Isabelle's house, Robert was impressed by the hominess of the place. There was a table with two chairs off to one side of the hearth and Robert noted the iron pot keeping warm on the flagstones.

Two wooden bowls had been laid on the table, along with two wooden spoons of intricate carved design. There seemed to be two of everything, which made sense if Isabelle had lived here with her mother. It was a good thing Bear was already gone or Robert suspected Isabelle would have gone without, while she insisted they ate from her only place settings.

"Please have a seat," she said calmly, as if she was trying to remember how to entertain guests. Robert cringed inwardly, realizing this poor waif had probably not had much friendship from those in the village.

Robert took the seat farthest from the hearth. It was a chilly morning and she was wearing long sleeves and a shawl. Even so, the fabric was thin and she was probably cold. She would benefit more from the heat of the fire, and it was his impulse to want to see to her comfort.

He watched her graceful movements as she served him the lion's share of the oats. When she sat across from him with her own small portion, Robert reached into his pouch and removed a small wrapped bundle of dried berries.

"I think these would go nicely with the oats, don't you?" he asked, producing the treat. He saw the way her eyes lit.

"They are out of season," she observed quietly. "And they aren't abundant in the forest around here, though I like them tremendously. I tried to cultivate a bush in my garden, but it never took. I don't have the same way with plants that my mother had."

"Then you shall have them all," Robert decided, pouring the small scoop of purple berries he'd had left, directly into her bowl, over her protests. Left with no choice, she accepted the gift with good grace.

The dried berries plumped up nicely when they came into contact with the hot, wet oats. Robert saw the enjoyment on her face as she took a bite and the burst of flavor from the berries hit her tongue.

Of course, his mind strayed to other things he would like to do with her tongue, but it was too soon. They had a long way to go before he would broach any sort of intimacy with Isabelle. For one thing, he had to be sure she understood the full implications of mating with a dragon knight.

When it came down to it, she was too important. He didn't want to screw this up. He wanted forever with her—but only if she could handle all that was expected of a woman sharing her life with two knights and their dragon partners.

It was nice to have company again, Isabelle thought. After sharing breakfast with her, Robert had stayed near the house, working on the barn and insisting on going with her when she went down to the river to fetch water. Growloranth went with them too, and much to her surprise, he took a swim downstream in the river while she and Robert filled the water vessels they had brought with them.

Robert had insisted on bringing more jugs and buckets than she usually used to carry water, noting that his group had used up most of her reserves—even the buckets and barrels she had set out to catch rainwater last night. Apparently dragons were thirsty creatures.

But Growloranth more than made up for it by hauling all the filled water jugs back to her house. She enjoyed watching the dragon. He was so perfectly suited to this environment, his coloration making him hard to see against the dark forest.

In fact, until he'd moved, she'd had a hard time spotting him as he lay on the bank of the river, drying off after his swim.

Between Growloranth's ability to hide in plain sight in the forest, and his mate's undeniable resemblance to the sky, she began to suspect this pair of dragons was a little out of the ordinary. The few times she had seen other dragons fly over the village and forest on their routine patrols of the border, they had stood out against the sky in vibrant colors, their scales sparkling in the sun. By contrast, she noted that Growloranth didn't seem especially interested in polishing his scales, though he had that same metallic sheen to his hide that all dragons seemed to share. He just kept the surface of his scales somewhat duller than she expected—possibly to blend in even better with his surroundings.

And Robert moved very quietly for such a big man. She barely even heard him walk when he was right beside her. It made her think he was a bit more than just a regular knight— if there was such a thing as a *regular* knight. She had never met a knight before Robert and Bernard, but they both seemed rather special to her.

Robert worked near the house all day. While she tended to the normal chores of washing up and sweeping out the house, he seemed to be perpetually busy working on the barn. She had known the place was in bad shape, but beyond basic repairs, she couldn't do much about the sagging walls of the old structure. Luckily for her, Robert and even his dragon, seemed to think fixing up her barn was a good use of their time.

Not that she really needed the barn anymore. While her mother had been alive, they had kept a few animals, but the stock was all gone after last year's especially tough winter. She missed caring for her own animals, but occasionally her skills as a healer were called for by those in the village. She was known for bandaging sore legs, mending broken wings and the like.

The folk in the village might not like her, but they used her skills when they needed them. Which was a good thing for her as well. The villagers often paid for her work with food items she couldn't forage or grow for herself, supplementing her meager supplies.

Robert and she shared the midday meal in her newly swept home. He insisted on providing the food from his own rations, and she dined on a hard cheese the likes of which she had never tasted before. He also had sweetened nuts and smoked jerky, which made a strange but filling meal.

Afterward, Growloranth announced he was going hunting. *"After all..."* the dragon said into her mind, *"...we like to pay our way, and my knight has a proposition to put to you, mistress."* Growloranth gave Robert a very significant look with those giant, jeweled eyes of his before walking into the forest and just disappearing.

"For such a big creature, he walks like a shadow in the forest. You can't even see a leaf move when he passes," Isabelle observed, watching after the dragon. "Amazing."

"He has many skills," Robert agreed as he stood next to her near the barn. "As for the proposition he mentioned..." The knight seemed to hesitate before turning to meet her gaze. "We all talked this over last night and we would like to ask if we could remain here, in your barn, for a few days. It would make a good base of operations for us while we pursue our mission, and we would pay you for putting us up, of course, but there is one catch."

She was very interested to hear the catch, but she'd had some inkling that they wanted to stay by the way Robert hung around and fixed the place up. If they were moving on, they likely wouldn't have spent any time on her dilapidated barn, and Robert and Growloranth would have been long gone, following in the path of their two companions.

"So what's the catch?" she asked, gazing up into his charming brown eyes.

He really was a handsome devil. If she wasn't careful, she could spend quite a bit of her time fantasizing about what it would be like to have a man like him in her life. What would it be like, she wondered idly, to be the wife of a knight? To be a true lady? With all that entailed...

She dismissed the thought with a little pang of regret. She was no lady. She might have been taught the manners of a more gently-bred girl, but in truth, Isabelle was nothing and no one. She lived on the edge of survival in a hut on the edge of the forest, near a village full of people who wouldn't spit on her if she were on fire. Her existence was tenuous, at best. Right now, she could only live day to day, never certain of how she would get through the next day, the next week, the next month. She had no business dreaming of being this knight's lady.

"You may have noticed that we've been trying to keep our presence here unnoticed," Robert went on, oblivious to her inner conjecture. "We would like you to keep it to yourself, should any of the villagers come here, or you go there. We don't want anyone to know we're in the area. Your barn provides a good vantage point and base for our work on the border, but we need to keep it secret."

"I have little contact with the villagers at this time of year. And I see no reason why I would tell anyone of your presence here. No matter my mother's origins, I am a loyal citizen of Draconia, and I know the dragons and knights that protect the border are to be trusted. I have trust in you and your dragon partners—that you're doing good work here, and I won't interfere. I will not tell anyone you're here. I swear it." She spoke the last words like a vow and he seemed to take her at her word.

"Thank you, milady," Robert said formally. "We will only be here for a few days at most, but we will try not to be a burden. And we can perhaps make your life a bit easier by doing as I have done today—fixing things and providing supplies. We will also leave you with a purse of coins and whatever else we can spare from our supplies when we go. And you will have the thanks of ourselves and our Lair. If you ever need anything, you can always go to the Border Lair for help. Anyone who can commune with dragons is welcome there."

This was more than she expected and his words touched her deeply. She felt a little choked up but strove for calm as she thanked him again and turned back to her home. If Growloranth was bringing meat for dinner, she was going to be ready to cook it into something delectable, if at all possible.

CHAPTER THREE

Growloranth provided a side of venison later that
afternoon that he had already butchered and dressed. The
dragon's sharp claws made short work of such things, and
were even delicate enough to skin the beast so the hide could
be cured.

The dragon and his knight must have been busy retrieving
the previous day's skin from the forest as well, because when
she looked in the back of the barn, there were two deer hides
stretched on newly constructed frames, drying. Those hides,
if she worked them a bit more, could be fashioned into winter
clothing or even a blanket to keep her warm this winter. She
might also be able to trade them in the village for food or
other supplies.

The thoughtfulness of the knight and his dragon was
beyond measure. Not only were they making sure the roof of
her barn wouldn't fall in this winter, they were also providing
a means for her survival beyond their departure from her
home. Tears filled her eyes when she saw the evidence of
their kindness.

"I can smoke this for you, so it will stay good for quite a while,"
Growloranth offered, holding up a large cut of the meat.

"Are you sure? Doesn't that take a long time?" Isabelle
asked, concerned that the dragon not put himself out too

much on her behalf.

"*Since Robert tells me we're staying overnight, it actually is a simple process,*" Growloranth told her. "*We tie the meat to the rafters of the barn directly over my head, with a wrap to catch the juices so I don't end up wearing them.*" He paused to send up a smoky, dragonish chuckle. "*In the night as I breath, the smoke will cook and cure the meat over several hours. By morning, you should have a number of well-smoked cuts that will last a long time, if you take care with them.*"

"That's ingenious," she marveled at the dragon's ingenuity. "I would love that, if you truly don't mind."

"*It would be my pleasure,*" Growloranth stated. "*We will do this every night we're here so that when we go, you will be well-stocked with meat for the coming cold. It is the least we can do to help repay your generosity.*"

Moved to tears again, Isabelle could only try to smile her thanks as she took the bits of meat she was going to use tonight, and made a run for the house. She hoped the dragon understood and realized she could send him her thoughts without the risk of tears.

"*I cannot thank you enough, Sir Growloranth,*" she told him mind-to-mind. "*It has been so long since anyone thought of my welfare, I'm afraid my emotions are getting the better of me. Please excuse my flight. It's silly to weep over such kindness.*"

"*I weep for the thoughtlessness of your neighbors that has brought you to such a crossroads, my dear,*" Growloranth answered in a kindly rumble in her mind. "*You should not live in such a place with such mean people. If Robert has not made it clear, you will always be welcome at the Lair. I would take you there myself, if you but say the word. We would love to have you become part of our little community.*"

"*Thank you, truly, Sir Growloranth, but I'm afraid I cannot bring myself to leave here just yet. You see, my mother is buried here. And this house reminds me of all the good times she and I shared. All of her belongings are still here, and I sense her presence in every room. In every whisper of the wind against these walls. It's too soon for me to give her up.*"

"*I do understand, milady,*" Growloranth said quietly. "*Losing someone you love is not an easy thing. When I lost my first knight,*"

Kinneth, I went into mourning for two decades. He was such a good man. So decent and strong of mind and limb. He was the companion of my youth and I will always miss his presence in my life. It was a long time before I could even think about joining my life to another knight. Finally, it was Tildeth who talked me around to trying again." He paused, seeming to consider his words. *"You see, we dragons live much longer than our knights and it is a serious matter to put ourselves into a situation where we will, in all likelihood, outlive the man we choose to bond with—over and over again. But in the end, there is much to be gained from the risk. We protect our land and peoples, and we have the chance to live a life that's full of love and laughter, pain, yes, and triumph at times. We share in our knights' lives and are better for it. Without the risk, there is no reward. And without the pain of loss, we would never have loved. It is a double-edged sword, but one we all must take up at some point, to truly live."*

Isabelle thought about his words for a long moment as she sat at her kitchen table, wiping her teary eyes. *"You are a wise being, Sir Growloranth."*

Isabelle cooked a savory stew that night, using a few of the onions she had grown in her garden that year and stored in the cold storage bin dug into the floor of the house. She also used some of the herbs and tubers she had gathered from the forest earlier in the year.

Sir Bernard and Tildeth came back as the sun went down, walking in from the forest instead of landing in full sight of the village. Isabelle understood how easily the dragon would be seen if they had chosen to land out in the open. She was too light in color, too sparkly. To avoid being seen, they had landed in the forest and walked to Isabelle's place under cover of the trees.

Tildeth and Growloranth twined their long necks in greeting and disappeared within the dark barn. Isabelle had seen Growloranth return from another foray into the forest with another deer while she was cooking dinner and she expected that one was meant for the dragons. But sure enough, when she went outside to fetch a small piece of wood from the barn a while later, Robert was working on another deer hide, attaching it to another newly-made frame. Bernard and Robert spent a short while talking quietly and cleaning up from their labors. As night fell in earnest, a knock sounded on her door and she let them into her small house. Both sported wet hair and fresh clothing. They wore dark colors in well-worn fabrics that allowed them to move even more silently than before. They also looked neat and comfortable. And incredibly handsome.

Bernard had shed his bulky leather armor and she could see now that he was built of solid muscle. Leaner than she had expected for such a big man, she could see the muscles of his arms rippling as he moved. Her mouth watered at the sight. Never had she been so close to two such handsome men.

Of the two, Robert had the more perfectly formed face. His hair was slightly longer than Bear's, and he was a tiny bit smaller in stature than his fighting partner. Bear was a mountain of a man who spoke little, but watched all. He had a penetrating gaze, and if his face wasn't quite as perfect as Robert's, he was still just as attractive, just in a different way.

Robert was gorgeous. Bear was compelling. And both made her knees weak when they moved close to her in the confines of the small house.

"Do you play?" Sir Bernard asked, shaking her out of her reverie. He was pointing toward the small stringed instrument in the far corner of the room.

"My mother taught me," Isabelle informed him. "We brought that with us from her homeland far in the north. She also played the flute and tin whistle, which she taught me as well. We used to pass the time during the cold winter months practicing by the fire."

She remembered those long winter nights fondly. Her mother had been a truly gifted musician, but she refused to play for the villagers—and had forbidden Isabelle from doing so as well. In honor of her mother's memory, Isabelle still kept that promise to this day.

"Mayhap you'll play for us after dinner?" Robert asked with a hopeful look in his eyes. "Bear plays the flute quite well. Perhaps you can find a song you both know."

Isabelle looked at Sir Bernard. He seemed a bit bashful, but willing to try, so she nodded.

"We can try," she answered gamely, motioning for the men to sit at the table.

There were only two chairs and they hesitated, looking at each other for a moment before Sir Bernard inexplicably rushed out the door. Before she could ask where he'd gone, he was back, a heavy log in his hands. He carried the huge chunk of tree easily, impressing Isabelle with his strength. The piece had been cut to a suitable height, she realized when he placed it upright at one side of the table. He could use it as a stool, solving the seating issue.

"I was going to sit by the hearth," she said quietly. "But this is much better. Thank you for thinking of it."

Bear smiled as he sat on the up-ended log, and she and Robert took the chairs. She was seated at the one next to the hearth, so she could easily reach the pot of stew. She lifted it off the hook that had kept it bubbling over the fire, and placed the heated pot in the center of the table, on a block of wood designed to hold it steady and protect the table top from its heat.

She uncovered the iron pot and the aroma of the stew spilled forth. It smelled good. Better than anything she had cooked in a long time. She didn't usually go to much trouble just for herself. Since her mother's death, there were precious few reasons to cook a special meal.

"That smells delicious," Robert complimented her as she reached for the two wooden bowls she and her mother had used.

She filled both, handing one to Bear, but when it came time for her to give the other one to Robert, he instead offered another wooden bowl of different design. He smiled at her, softening the realization that he had noticed that she didn't own much in the way of tableware.

"We have things in our packs that we can use to supplement your wares," he said quietly. "I know you live simply and have little use for company." She was shamed by his knowledge of her lack of friends. "We have imposed on your hospitality a great deal and you have not complained once, though you have had a right to." He laughed and held the bowl steady as she filled it for him, letting the moment pass.

It was embarrassing to know they had noticed how poorly she lived, but their matter-of-factness about it made her feel a little better. They were truly gentlemen as well as knights of the realm.

"Mama and I didn't entertain much. We only made what we needed for ourselves," she tried to explain in a quiet voice as she filled his bowl.

"Made?" Bear asked. "You made these things?" He held up the intricately carved spoon, seeming to admire the woodwork she had taken pains to learn how to do competently.

This, at least, was a question she could answer without shame. She put down the wooden ladle as Robert placed his now-full bowl down in front of him. Then she reached into her pocket and pulled out her latest project. It was the little piece of wood she had taken from the barn's small stockpile earlier in the day.

"I began working on this today. It will take a while yet to finish the fine detail and smooth it out so there is no fear of splinters, but your presence here reminded me that I should at least try to be prepared for company." She offered the half-carved spoon to Bear for his inspection. The spoon form was complete. It was the scrollwork and leaf pattern on the stem she had yet to fill in completely.

"This is fine work, mistress. You have great skill with wood carving. Why, you could trade these for coin in many towns and villages," Bear proclaimed, examining the spoon with great care.

Isabelle smiled. "I actually do trade them on occasion.

35

There is a tinker that comes through once every season. He does not leave without visiting me to see what I have to trade. He was here last month and I traded a set of twelve spoons of similar design for my new bed linens and a few copper pennies. I would have had more to trade except it was harvest and I had little time to work on them," she admitted. "I used the pennies to buy eggs each market day, until they ran out."

"You like eggs?" Bear asked quietly, handing the half-finished carving back to her.

"Very much," she agreed, pocketing the spoon and realizing they had yet to begin their meal. It seemed the knights were waiting for her. "Do you mind if we say the blessing before we eat?" she asked, not sure of the proper etiquette.

"By all means," Robert answered, smiling and putting her at ease.

She paused, bowing her head. "Blessed Mother of All, it is by your bounty that we have this food to eat. Thank you for your blessing. By your grace, please watch over us and guide us with your loving hand, this we pray," she said, using the simple words her mother had often used.

There were more formal blessings, but on this occasion it seemed only right to use the more familiar words. They put her at ease, regardless of the fact that she was about to share yet another meal with two of the most attractive men she had ever met.

But they were not for her. These men were noble. Knights of the realm. She was just a poor woman who eked out a living on the edge of the forest. She was nobody. She could never hope to claim the attention of a man such as these in a romantic way. Still…a girl could dream.

Blessing complete, they started to eat in comfortable silence. From the way the men devoured the stew, she gathered they liked it. A lot. When she was only halfway through her own portion, they were already finishing theirs. Bear finished first, looking at her with a somewhat sheepish expression.

"This is delicious, mistress," he said, watching her with hopeful eyes. It was odd to her how much a grown man—a knight, no less—could seem like a youngling at times.

"Please do not stand on ceremony. If you want more, take it. With all the meat your companions have set to smoke tonight, there will be a bounty in my larder tomorrow the likes of which it has never seen before. I thought perhaps, if you liked the stew, you and Sir Robert would finish this pot tonight. Will that be enough?" She looked uncertainly at her small pot and then back at the big men who were eyeing the stew in it avariciously.

"It is more than enough," Robert assured her. "Thank you for thinking of our comfort."

She smiled and went back to eating as the men wrestled over dividing up the remainder of the stew. There was a small tussle, but they seemed to recall their surroundings before it could escalate into anything bigger. Isabelle hid her smile, bending her head to eat.

The more she was around these knights, the more she liked them. She was beginning to see them as individuals. As men, with all the idiosyncrasies of other people. They were real to her in a way they hadn't been before.

She knew that Bear—Sir Bernard—kept many of his thoughts to himself, but he thought deeply. She saw evidence that Sir Robert had deep respect for the quieter man and often sought his counsel before deciding on a course of action. Sir Robert was also very sharp-witted and although glib of tongue, he was kind-hearted.

The dragons too, were fascinating individuals. Isabelle could see the love and respect between the male and female dragon, and the deep bond they shared with their knights. Each respected the other, and the quartet was a highly-functioning unit, aligned in purpose and matched in skills and temperament.

She never would have guessed anything like that about knights and their dragons before meeting these four. She felt blessed to have crossed their path, and doubly blessed by the small things they were doing for her around the homestead that would make the long, cold winter so much easier to bear.

After dinner, they coaxed her to play a few tunes with Bear. They knew a few common songs and were able to do passable duets while Robert hummed along, smiling and tapping his foot.

The dragons moved closer to listen, much to Isabelle's surprise. She saw the sky blue of Lady Tildeth's hide out her back window and realized Sir Growloranth had been watching from the side of the house for some time when he opened his eye and winked at her through the side window. If he hadn't moved, she would not have been able to see him against the dark night outside. He was just that stealthy.

Sadly, the evening had come to an end when she couldn't contain a yawn. The men noticed right away and made their departure. It was kind of them to consider the fact that she'd had a very long day, but in a way, she would rather have spent more time enjoying their company.

As she washed the few dishes and set them to dry, she thought of the lovely evening they had spent together. Perhaps they would have another dinner like this tomorrow night. She could but hope. It was so rare for her to have guests—and never had she had such amusing guests.

In fact, she hadn't had this much fun since her mother had died. That thought brought to mind all she had lost when her mother had passed, and she couldn't help the tears that clogged her throat and fell into the dishwater.

"She is crying again," Growloranth grumbled to the knights as if it was their fault.

They were all back in the barn except the well camouflaged male dragon. He was on guard duty, watching from the shadows outside Isabelle's house. He could easily see into her window and was reporting her movements back to the men in the barn.

"I don't like how alone she is," Tildeth observed, compassion in her tone.

"We cannot leave her here like this," Growloranth stated.

"We also can't force her to go," Robert reminded them all. *"We will have to work on convincing her. She has memories here that are obviously hard for her to let go of."*

"Sometimes it's better to leave the memories behind and begin new ones," Growloranth said in a subdued tone.

Robert remembered that dragons went off on their own to mourn, most of the time, after losing their knight. Growloranth and Tildeth had both lost their first knights and spent time in the mountains, grieving. They had not stayed in the Lair where their former knights had lived and worked. In fact, when they came back, they did not even go to that Lair, but instead, asked for assignment to the Border Lair after choosing their new knight partners.

"Dragons can be far smarter than humans when it comes to such things," Robert observed.

"This place is all she knows," Bear put in. *"She does not think she has any alternative, and she fears leaving the known behind for the unknown."*

Robert was impressed with Bear's grasp of the situation. He nodded at his fighting partner as they settled down for the night in the barn. Growloranth would be on watch outside in the shadows that were his element.

"Maybe we can show her a little bit of what we can offer her at the Lair," Robert mused. *"After we complete our mission, we could invite her for a visit, if we haven't convinced her by then."*

The others agreed and conversation drew to a close for the night as Tildeth and the knights fell asleep. Growloranth would wake them if anything happened.

A few hours later, in the deepest part of the night, Growloranth's voice sounded in Robert's mind, waking him instantly.

"A man is coming up the path in haste."

"I'll be there in a minute." Robert promised, already slipping his sword and dagger from their scabbards as he made his way through the dark barn.

39

"He just rushed right past me," Growloranth reported. *"Didn't even look in my direction. He's knocking on Isabelle's door."*

Robert could hear the loud raps on the wooden door, followed by the fellow speaking loudly enough to be heard in the barn and beyond.

"Isabelle, you've got to come. Mantell's prize bull is sick something awful. Mantell's stockman tol' me to come get you."

Robert reached the shadows by the door to the barn in time to see Isabelle answer her door. She was wearing her cloak and had a large bag slung across her body.

"I'll come, Darel, but this is an awful time of night to be asking favors. If the animal is so sick, why didn't he send for me before now?" Robert watched from the shadows as she closed her door behind her, then glanced at the barn while the townsman was already starting back down the path ahead of her, grumbling. He hadn't even glanced at the dragon.

Robert saw Growloranth wink at Isabelle. Her startled smile before she turned to follow the man was just the tiniest bit mischievous.

Robert waited for her to go down the path a bit before he came out of the barn. *"I'll take it from here, friend,"* he told Growloranth as he passed him, already on the trail of Isabelle and the stranger who had come for her in the night.

Robert tailed the odd duo all the way to the grand house he and Bear had discovered earlier. All the activity seemed to be centered around the barn, which was too well lit for him to infiltrate. However, there were windows, and the far side of the building was bathed in darkness. And if that didn't work out, there was always the roof.

Robert made his approach from the outside, on the dark side of the building, after watching Isabelle and the man—who was some kind of servant—enter the big barn. It took him a few moments to find a good vantage point, by which time Isabelle could be heard talking in soothing tones to both the people in the barn and the animal she had been fetched to treat.

When he finally got a good look at the situation, Robert didn't like what he saw. The animal in question was indeed a big bull. He was stomping and snorting, pawing the ground with a wild look in his eye. Several people stood around the beast's heavily-fenced stall, but nobody seemed brave enough to go in there with him.

Isabelle would have to, if she was going to treat the animal, and that worried Robert immensely. The beast could crush her or gore her, in no time at all.

But then she began to whisper something to the aggressive animal. The bull's ears perked up and he gradually quieted as she entered his stall. Robert watched in awe as she gentled the massive creature and even convinced him to allow her to examine him. She ran her hands over his belly and down his legs. The creature seemed to revel in her touch and even tried to lick her a few times, following her movements with its gaze.

The bull followed her like a pet dog when she moved toward the rail to speak with one of the men who watched from afar. She spoke calmly, in a firm voice that didn't seem to upset the bull, but Robert saw her put her hand on the bull's forehead when the man spoke, seeming to calm the creature with her touch.

After a few words were exchanged, Isabelle moved away from the rail and dug in her bag for a bundle of dried herbs. Robert saw the older man send a younger one out of the barn on an errand, and a few moments later, a bucket of water had been brought in and handed over the rail to Isabelle. She crumbled her herbs into the bucket of water and stirred, the bull watching her actions with seeming adoration.

When she stepped back, she led the bull to the bucket and Robert watched in amazement as it lapped up the herb and water mix with what looked like bovine pleasure—if there was such a thing. Not long after, the bull's eyelids started to droop and Isabelle coaxed the creature to lie down on his side.

She sat with him, petting him and speaking in low, gentle tones, until the bull seemed to fall asleep. At that point, she delved into her bag again and pulled out a stoppered bottle with some kind of oil inside. She poured the entire bottle of dark oil onto the bull's belly and rubbed it in.

Now that the creature was lying down, even Robert could see the reddened patches on its hide, particularly on its belly, where Isabelle was applying her medicine. She followed the oil with a salve and then bathed the surrounding area with a green gooey substance she had taken from her bag.

By the time she was done, the bull's underside was a blotchy concoction of many colors—mostly green, brown and yellow—but the animal looked at peace, and as if he would stay that way for quite a while. Isabelle patted the creature's head once more before she left his stall, pausing to speak with the older male, who was probably the stable master. She gave this man a few more things out of her bag, and pointed to each one as she issued what had to be instructions.

After that, she seemed to deflate, yawning hugely as she walked—alone—to the barn door. Robert ghosted around the outside of the building so he could watch her progress. He couldn't believe nobody was going to walk her home. It was still pitch dark out. Anything could be prowling out in the darkness.

And in fact, Robert soon realized the dark shape on the roof of the barn was Growloranth. Apparently the dragon didn't want to leave Isabelle's safety in the hands of a mere human. Robert had to suppress a chuckle. Growloranth, it seemed, was becoming as attached to the lady as his knight.

Isabelle began walking slowly toward her home, but the back door to the great house opened and a dark-clad woman rushed out. She held a wrapped bundle out to Isabelle and Robert could see Isabelle's expression brighten for a moment when she accepted the small parcel. The other woman rushed back into the house and Isabelle went on her way, alone.

Except, she wasn't really alone. Robert and Growloranth

shadowed her steps all the way back to her place on the edge
of the woods.

CHAPTER FOUR

After the nocturnal excursion, Bear and Tilly decided they had to run an errand before their morning patrol began. Robert slept while Growloranth kept watch, though nothing else exciting happened for the little that remained of the night.

Bear and Tilly returned shortly after dawn with a huge sack of provisions and a surprise for Isabelle. Robert smiled when he saw what his fighting partner had done. Sometimes Bear had really excellent ideas, and this was definitely one of them.

Bear and Tilly stuck around for breakfast, which Robert totally understood. Bear, no doubt, wanted to see Isabelle's face when she realized what he'd brought for her.

He got his chance about a half hour later when Isabelle came outside to the barn. She seemed hesitant to enter, but once she saw the men were up and about, she came inside...and then stopped quite still.

"Do you like them?" Bear asked, moving close to Isabelle as she saw what he'd done.

"Are they for me?" she whispered, apparently very moved by the gesture.

Bear walked with her over to the wooden cages he and Tilly had brought in earlier. Inside were a small flock of chickens. Two hens and one rooster. From there, she would be able to breed more and have plenty of eggs for herself, as well as some to trade or sell.

"I tried to get a few more hens, but the farmer wouldn't part with more than two," Bear said somewhat sheepishly.

"Sir Bernard..." Isabelle began, clearly choked up at the gesture. "I am overwhelmed. Are you certain they are for me? It is too much."

Bear seemed relieved as a grin broke over his face. "They are most definitely for you, milady. I only wish I could have talked the farmer out of more of his flock. And after I do my patrol, I will build a coop for you on the warm side of your home, so they will be safe through the winter. I come from a farming family and we kept our coop on the other side of the kitchen wall where the chimney was. As long as you leave a small fire burning in the kitchen hearth, the chickens on the other side of the chimney will benefit from the warmth all winter."

A tear rolled down her face, followed by another and another and then she did something unexpected. She literally launched herself into Bear's arms. Taken by surprise, he nonetheless was smart enough to wrap his arms around her, accepting her hug and the kisses she bestowed on his rough cheek.

Bear turned his head and one of her kisses landed on his lips. She stilled, moving back slightly to look into his eyes while Robert and the dragons held their breath. What she did next would determine a lot about the future.

When she stayed motionless in Bear's arms, Bear did what came naturally, moving closer, slowly, giving her the opportunity to flee...but she didn't. She waited, seemingly unsure but willing to trust him as he lowered his mouth to hers, giving her a proper kiss. A proper kiss that turned improper within only a few moments.

And she...she just seemed to...surrender. That was as good a word as any when all the tension fled her small body and she returned Bear's kiss with a passion that looked as fiery as it was unexpected. Robert watched with both joy and a bit of envy as his fighting partner was the first to claim a kiss from the woman they intended to make their own.

There would be time for Robert to kiss her though—if everything proceeded according to the plan they had mapped out deep in the night. They had strategized how to woo her. The first step was to continue to fix up her home and shower her with small gifts that would make her life better, even if she chose finally not to take them up on their offer of marriage and a home in the Lair.

Truth to tell, even if she rejected them, the offer of a home in any dragon Lair would stand. If Robert and Bear couldn't convince her she was the one for them, perhaps another pair of knights would be luckier. Or she could work with the dragons for the rest of her life. Her pure heart and the ability to speak to dragonkind, paired with her lack of fear of them guaranteed her acceptance among them, even if she didn't want to mate a pair of knights.

It might just break Robert's heart to see her go to someone else, though. He already had deep feelings for the girl, and he suspected she was the one meant to complete their family—no one else's.

When Bear finally let go of Isabelle, by slow degrees, gentling the kiss that had raged for long minutes, her eyes were deliciously dazed. There was no doubt she had enjoyed Bear's kiss. It was only when reality returned that she panicked, and a flush of becoming pink graced her cheeks.

"Oh, dear," she breathed, stepping back from Bear. He let her go, dropping his arms, but watching her carefully. As did they all.

"I am sorry if I moved too fast," Bear said quietly. "But I do want you to know I admire you a great deal. I would like to court you when our mission is done, with an eye toward seeing if you could perhaps live with Tilly, Growloranth, Robert and me. We have all talked about it, and we suspect you may be the one who might complete our family."

"Too fast, Bear," Robert warned silently. *"You're overwhelming*

the lass."

"*No, look at her face.*" Tildeth cut in on the mental conversation that included only the two dragons and two knights. "*She is thinking about it. Under the panic, she is tempted.*"

Robert noted the way Isabelle looked at each one of them, first the dragons, one by one, then meeting Robert's gaze with only a hint of wide-eyed disbelief. Tilly was right. Under the fear was…interest.

"*Hot damn,*" Robert observed to his friends. "*I think you're right. Good work, Bear. Although I'm still jealous as hell that you got to kiss her first. Tell me, is she as sweet as I imagine?*"

"*Even sweeter,*" Bear confirmed. "*And far hotter than I ever dreamed. She will set us both aflame should we ever convince her to be our mate.*"

"*I pray the Mother of All will give us the chance,*" Robert replied, sending the prayer heavenward even as he smiled encouragingly at Isabelle.

"And you, Sir Robert?" Isabelle said softly, a slight tremor in her voice. "Do you also believe this?"

Robert stepped forward and took her hand in his, looking deep into her eyes. "I do." He dipped to place a chaste kiss on her brow, unwilling to scare her off. Her world had just been rocked, judging by the look in her eyes. He didn't want to add even more chaos. "I think you are a courageous, clever, lovely woman with much to offer our family. You could complete us. All we ask is that you think about it." He let go of her hands and moved slightly away. "As Bear said, we have a mission to complete, but after we're done with that, we would like you to think about visiting the Lair with us to see how we live, and what it's like being among so many dragons and knights. It is our hope that you'll like what you see and perhaps it will help convince you that we have only the best intentions where you are concerned."

She was silent a long moment, until she finally answered. "I would like to see it someday. For now, you've given me a great deal to think about." She looked at the cages holding the quietly clucking hens. "And a flock of chickens to feed."

She smiled and Robert breathed a sigh of relief. They were past the biggest hurdle. She hadn't turned them down outright. She was just being cautious—and who could blame her? She hadn't survived this long on her own without being careful.

Isabelle turned and, while she didn't actually flee, she certainly moved rather quickly out the door of the barn and back to her house. Robert had to smile when she sent back a message via Growloranth, apparently unwilling to talk mind-to-mind with anyone but the dragon at the moment.

"Lady Isabelle invites you to breakfast when you are ready," Growloranth conveyed the message to Robert and Bear with a comically haughty air. *"And may I add my congratulations on your swift thinking, Sir Bernard. All along I thought my knight was quicker with the ladies, but I see I have underestimated your prowess. Well done, and thank you for moving things along. The sooner you find your mate, the sooner my lady and I can take to the sky. While we are not pressuring you to hurry, just the same, we are glad you are showing signs of bringing your search to an amiable end. Tildeth and I agree that Lady Isabelle would make a wonderful addition to our little family."*

"It will be nice to have another female to help with the little ones when they come along," Tildeth put in. *"Isabelle is a gentle soul who would be kind to younglings of either race. And she would sing the sweetest lullabies."* Tildeth sounded almost wistful.

Robert knew that parenting of babies was shared by the mixed families in most Lairs. The humans acted as a second set of parents to any baby dragon born in the family, while the dragons did the same for any human children. It was an arrangement that had been working for centuries within the borders of Draconia, and Robert looked forward to seeing it in action in his own small family unit—once they found their mate. He would bet his best suit of armor that Isabelle was the one. Now they just had to convince her of that little fact.

They walked to the house, Bear carrying the heavy sack of provisions he had secured on his early morning flight. The farmer from whom he'd bought the chickens had sold him a lot more besides the livestock. Robert was glad Bear had been so thoughtful, but he felt like a dolt by comparison. He had yet to shower their lady with gifts, but for the life of him, he couldn't think of what he could give her besides his heart. And he didn't think she was ready yet to hear declarations of undying love from a man she had met only a day before.

When Isabelle let them into her home, Bear took the lead, placing the heavy sack of supplies on the counter near the washbasin. It was a smart move because, as Robert quickly realized, Isabelle had already prepared breakfast using her own supplies. Bear's provisions might hurt her feelings or cause embarrassment in light of her own meager offerings. The last thing they wanted to do was hurt her in any way. Leaving the supplies for later was the best course of action at that moment.

Bear smiled and rubbed his hands together in a gesture of anticipation as he settled on the tree stump he had brought in the night before. A large portion of cooked oat mash was already in the bowl placed in front of him. Robert was treated similarly when he sat, and they shared a companionable half hour eating and talking of simple things.

When it came time for Bear and Tildeth to get on their way, Bear placed a lingering kiss on Isabelle's cheek. He thanked her in the gentlest tone Robert had ever heard from his fighting partner. It was obvious Bear didn't want to leave, but they had come here to do a job and they wouldn't be able to truly court Isabelle until their mission was completed.

Bear nodded to him and left, going directly to Tilly, who waited deeper into the forest so she would not be seen by anyone from the village. Growloranth was closer, but Tilly's lighter coloring would make her stand out more against the greenery surrounding Isabelle's home.

"Take care of her. I'll be in touch when I have something to report," Bear sent to Robert silently as he disappeared into the forest.

"I've got the watch, partner. Good hunting," Robert sent back, aware in the corner of his mind that was connected to Bear through his connection with his dragon partner, that Tilly had already launched them both into the air.

Robert helped Isabelle clean up from their meal. After the dishes were washed and set to dry, he opened the large sack Bear had brought in earlier, putting things away in Isabelle's kitchen as if it was nothing out of the ordinary. He saw her wide eyes as he uncovered each new item. There were wheels of what looked like good, hearty cheese. Baskets of dried berries. Small jars of spices and salt. Larger flasks of oil and vinegar. Fruits that would keep well into the winter, and vegetables that would do likewise. The more perishable items Robert left out for Isabelle to deal with, since they would have to be used sooner.

"How long do you plan to stay," Isabelle asked, eyeing the mountain of food Robert had unpacked. Her gaze shot to his as she realized that her question could be thought of as rude. "I didn't mean—"

Robert held up his hands, palm outward as he smiled. "Be at ease, milady. We only have a few more days to complete our mission here, but we cannot in good conscience leave you anything but well-stocked for the winter."

"But this is all too much. The chickens were already too much, but this is…" She looked at the vast array of food items Bear had brought and seemed at a loss for words.

"This is only the beginning. Now that we know where you live, we will be back," Robert warned in a teasing tone. "Of course, you could always come with us when we leave. Women like you, who can speak with dragons and do not fear them, are always welcome in the Lair."

"You said something like that before, but what would I do? How would I earn my keep?" She looked worried and uncomfortable. "What would be my role?"

Robert moved closer to her. "You could come back with us as our mate."

"Both of you?" She seemed shocked, which worried him. He had hoped she already understood.

"Yes." There was no way to sugar-coat it. He had to be honest with her about their intentions, even if it scared her off. He had to try to explain it better to her, so that she would understand. "We are bonded on a soul-deep level with our dragons. And our dragons are mates. They already have two children who are grown and have knights and mates of their own. Their first knights died many years ago, and both Tildeth and Growloranth mourned their loss for decades before returning to pick another set of knights—Bear and I— to share their lives with. The thing is, because of our bond, the dragons cannot consummate their relationship again until Bear and I have a mate of our own. The spillover from a dragon mating flight is intense, from all accounts. If the knights bonded to the two dragons do not have a mate of their own to share in the deep love and passion, it can drive them mad. Which is why the prohibition was instituted long ago, that bonded dragons cannot mate until their knights have found a woman of their own, to love and share their lives and passions."

"So until you and Sir Bernard have found such a woman, your dragon partners cannot come together," she repeated, seeking his confirmation.

Robert nodded. "They have been very patient with us, and they will wait as long as they need to, but the sooner we find our mate, the sooner they can be together again as mates. Bear and I think that maybe you could be the woman for us."

"Why only one woman? Why can't you each find a wife of your own?"

"It doesn't really work that way," Robert admitted. "And I'm not entirely sure of the reasons why. Having never experienced a dragon mating through the bond I share with Growloranth, I can only speculate. But from what the mated knights have said, the spillover running through the bond is too intense. Only the triad joining seems to account for the closeness needed between the knights while their dragon partners' passions are running through them."

"I have never considered such a relationship," Isabelle admitted. He admired her honesty, though it pained him to hear her words. "Frankly, I had given up on finding even one man who would be willing to have me as his wife—or that I would consider as a husband. To suddenly be faced with two men vying to share my affections, not to mention two amazing dragons who would be reunited if I agreed…" She ran a hand through her hair as she leaned back against the kitchen counter. "It's all very confusing and kind of unbelievable."

Robert moved closer. He didn't want to push her too fast, but she needed to know where he stood in no uncertain terms. Bear had made himself clear earlier that morning. Now it was time for Robert to do the same.

"It can be simple," he said softly, drawing her gaze as he stopped close in front of her. She looked up into his eyes and he felt his heart stutter. She was so delicately beautiful, she stole his breath. "It is said the Mother of All guides us in these matters, more than other men. Knights often know very quickly if they've met the woman meant for them. We feel it—in our hearts. In our souls. I felt something profound when I first saw you in the forest. I feel it every time I'm in your presence." He moved closer, putting his hands on the counter behind her, one on either side of her hips. When she didn't object, he moved closer still. "I've never been in love before," he admitted. "I would like the chance to discover if what I'm feeling could be that most magical of all feelings. You are a very special woman, Isabelle. I think it would be very easy to fall in love with you."

"Is that what it would be? Love?" she asked, whispering.

"If you agreed to be our mate, we would settle for nothing less. If you cannot love us—both of us—then we are not the knights for you. All we're asking is that you give us a chance." He whispered the last words against her lips as he moved in for the kiss he'd been craving ever since he first laid eyes on her.

He took it slow, simply rubbing his lips against hers at first, keeping the kiss delicate and gentle. He wanted to savor this first kiss. The first of many, he hoped.

When she didn't pull away, he deepened the kiss, his tongue seeking entry, which was granted, much to his satisfaction. From there, he took things one step at a time, taking on the unexpected role of teacher and coach. He could tell from her shy responses that she was unused to kissing, and that nearly tore a little hole in his heart. How could such a special, desirable woman not know how to kiss?

It was his honor and privilege to show her all the ways a simple movement of lips and tongues could spark the flame he hoped to fan to an inferno at some point. Not today, perhaps, but sometime soon...when she was ready. And when he and Bear weren't embroiled in the middle of a demanding covert mission.

It was incredibly difficult, they were learning, to properly court a woman when most of their attention had to be on their job. With any luck, they'd be able to finish their observations soon, give their report to their superiors and come back to put serious effort into luring Isabelle away from her cottage on the edge of the woods, to their home in the Lair.

Robert wrapped his arms around her, drawing her close to his body. She was so soft. So unbelievably feminine. So perfect.

Her small hands crept up to his shoulders and explored the sensitive area near his neck. He was wearing only a simple woven shirt this morning and he was truly glad there was so little between her seeking fingers and his skin. When one of her hands dipped inside his collar, he groaned, loving the feel of her touching him.

But the sound seemed to alarm her, and he cursed himself for having made it. He let her draw away, breaking the kiss, but he didn't let her out of his arms. She drew back, looking up at him, searching his gaze. Her cheeks were flushed and she had a dewy look in her eyes that made him want nothing more than to kiss her again, but he knew he shouldn't rush her.

"You are amazing, Isabelle," he whispered, wanting her to know just how special she was.

Her gaze widened and any insecurity he had seen there

disappeared. That she needed his reassurance, touched him deeply. She was innocent. Unsure of her own value. That was something he would do his best to change over the course of their relationship. He would tell her and show her every day, he vowed, just how special she truly was.

"I'm not used to—" she began, but he stilled her words by placing one finger gently across her lips.

"I know. I'm sorry I rushed things. My only defense is that I've been wanting to take you into my arms since the first moment I saw you. I'll respect any boundaries you set, Isabelle, but please don't ask me not to at least try to kiss you every time you give me the slightest chance." He smiled, hoping she understood the teasing nature of his words.

He mentally held his breath until she returned his smile with a shy one of her own. She seemed more stunned than alarmed, and he took that as a good sign. There was hope for them yet.

Robert stepped back. There was much to do today and he had pushed her far enough for one morning.

"Shall we see to your new flock of chickens?" he asked playfully, hoping she would want to work with him instead of letting him go off on his own.

Excitement lit her eyes when she remembered the feathered cluckers in the barn.

"Bear said he would build a coop," she said, recalling Bear's earlier words.

"He did, but there's no reason we can't give him a head start. He's not the only one familiar with the care and feeding of your new feathered friends. Plus, he's bound to be tired when he returns and I'd like to help. What do you say?"

"Why not? The sooner we get them settled in their new home, the happier they will be," she agreed and they headed for the door together.

The rest of the morning was spent deciding how big and exactly where they were going to place the coop. Robert kept in touch with Bear through the dragons and he knew Bear was fine with Robert helping get the project started. In fact, he was thankful. The winds aloft were fierce today and Bear was having to expend a lot of energy just to stay on Tilly's back. He would be wrung out by the time he got back if that sort of weather kept up.

Robert let Isabelle decide where to place things, only having to give her guidance a couple of times to set her on the right path. She decided on the style and shape of the coop and he built it while she played with, and pet her new chickens. They weren't the friendliest of creatures at the best of times, but Isabelle seemed to have a way with the critters.

She fed them and tried out names for them, finally deciding to call them Henrietta, Jazzleberry and Bob. He laughed when she explained that the rooster was named—in a way—for both Bear and Robert.

By noon he had the bare bones of the structure set up. Bear would be able to put his touches on the inner workings of the place. The hens would need nesting boxes and whatever comforts Bear had in mind. Robert had already installed a watering system that would allow Isabelle to use her kitchen window to feed cups of water down a little chute that led directly to a shallow vessel from which the chickens could drink. The water dish was kept near enough to the hearth bricks that the water wouldn't freeze over in the deep winter, as long as Isabelle kept the kitchen hearth warm.

Which reminded him of his plan to cut some wood for her this afternoon. They shared a quick lunch of bread and cheese with some of the fruits Bear had brought that morning, and then went on a little jaunt through the woods with Growloranth to help drag a rather massive dead tree Robert had noticed the day before, closer to Isabelle's home. The dragon brought it to a good spot behind her house where Robert and Growloranth could work on it without being seen by anyone.

Although it was an activity Growloranth seldom engaged in, he seemed to enjoy breaking the log into smaller pieces that Robert then turned into even more manageable bits that Isabelle could use in her fireplace. When Isabelle came around to the back of the house, after she had finished fussing over her new chickens for a bit, she stopped short.

"You did all this in just a couple of hours?" She walked slowly toward Robert and Growloranth, her gaze roaming back and forth over the massive wood pile they'd created for her.

"Having a giant dragon around is useful, on occasion," Robert allowed with a little bow toward his partner. Growloranth only snorted, little tendrils of smoke heading up toward the leafy canopy of the forest.

"This is enough for the whole winter!" she exclaimed, her eyes wide.

Robert said nothing as she came closer, looking around at the neatly stacked firewood. When she got close enough, he saw the tears in her eyes and he reached for her, wanting to comfort her. He put one arm around her shoulders.

"Why are you upset?" he asked as gently as he could. Women were mysterious creatures, this one doubly so. He had to tread lightly until he understood what made her cry.

"I'm not upset. I'm overwhelmed," she replied, turning to look at him, though she stayed close. Her wide, glistening eyes looked up at him and he was lost. He would do anything for this woman. Anything at all. "Thank you, Robert."

A little thrill went through him when she spoke his name in such a familiar way. The barriers between them were dropping one by one, and he was happy to see them fall.

"It was our pleasure to assure that you will be safe and warm through the cold months. We will not leave you here without being certain we have done as much as possible to assure your comfort. We all agreed."

"Thank you." She reached up and kissed his cheek, then lowered her head to his chest, staying in the warmth of his arms. Robert saw her look in Growloranth's direction. "And thank you, Sir Growloranth. I haven't known such kindness in a very long time."

"You will want for nothing," Robert vowed. "Now that I know you are in the world, I will do all I can to see to your comfort, whether you choose to stay here or whether you ultimately decide to come with us to live in the Lair." He bent down to kiss her hair. "You are very special to me. To all of us," he whispered, holding her close. "We would like to make you part of our family, in the fullness of time. But we all agreed that you should not be pressured in any way into making that decision. If you come to us, we want you to come knowing that it is not your only choice. We want you to choose us. To choose me. And Bear. And to share your life with all four of us."

She was silent a long moment, then spoke in a small voice. "I don't know if I can."

He gentled her, stroking her back with his hands in a soothing gesture. "It's all right. There is time yet to discover more about this situation. You need to get to know us better, and to understand exactly what it is we have to offer. And sadly, we are still on a mission. We have to complete our task and report back to our superiors at the Lair within the next few days."

"You're not like regular dragon knight teams, are you?" she asked, surprising him. It pleased him that the woman he wanted for a mate was both observant and intelligent.

"What makes you say that?" he asked, testing her a little, just to see what she would say.

She stepped back, out of his arms, to look up at him. "Sir Growloranth blends with the forest as if he were a tree. And Lady Tildeth is nearly invisible in the blue sky, which is no doubt why she and Bear fly all day while you stay here." Her words were quiet but challenging in a playful way that felt good. It wasn't often he got to talk with anyone about the work they did. "I see the way you and Sir Growloranth watch the village. And I know enough about the goings on in that village to guess why you might be interested in some of the residents and their dealings."

Now he was truly intrigued. He stepped closer to her, sensing she might have insights they could use. "What do you know?"

"Cleef Mantell is a thief, and probably a traitor too," she whispered.

CHAPTER FIVE

"Cleef Mantell," Robert repeated, trying the name out. "Is that the name of the man who lives in the mansion under the trees?" he asked urgently.

She nodded. "It was to his barn that I was summoned last night. But you know that, don't you? I thought I saw Sir Growloranth aloft as I was making my way back home. And I have a feeling you weren't far behind." She tilted her head as she looked up at him, challenging him to tell her the truth.

At that moment, he could've kissed her. Not only was she smart, but she was observant too. Could the Mother of All have picked a more perfect mate for him? He thought not.

"As Bear and Tilly scout the day, he and I..." Robert pointed toward the dragon lurking not far away in the woods, "...have the night. We heard the commotion and would never have let you walk home alone as those barbarians in the village allowed. In truth, we were watching over you from the moment you answered your door. We would not let anything happen to you, Isabelle."

A smile broke over her face that enchanted him. "That is so sweet," she said softly. "Thank you." And then she reached up, using his shoulder for balance, she stood on tiptoe and kissed him. Not a peck on the cheek this time, but a full-on lip lock that both surprised and pleased him

59

immensely.

She might be a novice at kissing, but she wasn't shy.

He wasn't sure how long they stayed that way. Truth to tell, Robert was enjoying himself too much to pay attention to something as mundane as time, but Growloranth finally broke them apart. He spoke into both their minds.

"I hate to interrupt, but my lady and her knight return. They bring news."

Isabelle drew back from his lips slowly, a slightly self-conscious smile curving her lips that made him grin in return. Bear walked into the small clearing behind Isabelle's house and his expression was grim. Tildeth stopped inside the perimeter of the trees where she twined her long, sinuous neck with Growloranth's in greeting.

"The news is not good," Bear said without preamble. He was removing his leather gloves as he walked. His riding armor were made of the lightest possible shade of leather, then stained slightly with the blue of special berries to match Tilly's hide as much as possible. "There is a sizeable force massing on the other side of the border. It looks like enough men to occupy this village and hold it, making it the foothold Skithdron needs to be able to launch further attacks. And worse, there are many skiths being herded toward the pass. They will be here within the next day. Two, at most."

"Skiths?" Isabelle sounded appropriately shocked.

"We must get word to the Lair immediately," Robert said, already moving toward the barn. "Isabelle, pack what you want to save, and get ready to fly. We're taking you to the Lair for safety. You can return here after the battle—if there's anything left—but you cannot stay here right now."

"Good. Because I'm not stupid enough to try to hold my own against a herd of skiths!" She ran for the house. "But we have to take my chickens," she shouted back over her shoulder, making Robert pause to smile just a little. He should have realized she wouldn't leave her new flock to suffer the degradations sure to come if a herd of skiths arrived en masse.

"It'll be dark enough soon for Growloranth and I to do some more reconnaissance," Robert said to Bear as they entered the barn and began to gather their gear. "You take Isabelle to the Lair while Growly and I do our work here tonight, then join you in the morning."

"If they don't send Tilly and me back out again before you get in," Bear added.

"I won't be surprised if they do. You're just about the only pair at the Lair right now that can fly across the border undetected by day. I'm sure they'll get some of the other dark dragons to fly tonight after you make your report, so we'll watch the village and see what we can learn about this Cleef Mantell."

"Good plan," Bear agreed, finishing his packing and turning toward the door. Robert followed, his own pack in his hands. He would set Growloranth up to fly at a moment's notice, leaving no trace of their presence—except perhaps the repairs to the barn, the pile of cut firewood, and the new chicken coop.

Trying not to panic, Isabelle packed as many of her mother's treasures as she could. She hated to leave the house they had worked so hard to fix up and maintain, but it had to be done. This flimsy place of wood and straw would never stand up against the massive size and strength of a skith. Snakelike and armed with massive jaws that could snap a person in two, skiths also had the charming ability to spit highly corrosive venom up to twenty feet away, or so it was said.

Isabelle had seen a skith from afar once, and that once was enough to cure her of ever wanting to see another. That one had been a stray that had come over the border all on its own. Word had been sent to the Border Lair and dragon patrols had been stepped up. For the next two days, Isabelle had seen several pairs of dragons and their knights crisscrossing the skies over where the skith had been seen until finally, they found their prey.

Flames had erupted in the night, just over the horizon. Word had come with the next sunrise that the stray skith had been eliminated.

Dragons were the most effective method of killing skiths, though groups of men had been known to fight them if there was no other alternative. Heavy casualties were to be expected if mere humans took on a skith. The highly corrosive venom could kill outright if left untreated long enough. Usually men who took on skiths and lived to tell the tale bore horrific scars from the acid burns as testament to their bravery.

Isabelle paused by the door of her home with her two big bags of her possessions, one in each hand. She looked back at the place that had once been a happy home shared with her beloved mother. Now it was a place of memory—cold and of only small comfort to a heart that yearned for warmth, care and love.

"I'm sorry, Mama," she said to the empty room, feeling her mother's presence there for perhaps the last time. She had never wanted to leave this way, but there was no alternative. To stay was to die. Her mother would not want that for her. Isabelle looked around the lonely home and thought she felt the benevolent understanding her mother had always given her. It was like her mother was acknowledging the rightness of her decision to leave. "I love you, mama. Always." Tears filled her eyes as she exited the house.

But Bear was there, waiting for her. He took her bags from her numb hands and looked searchingly behind her, concern on his dear face.

"Is this all you have? We can take more, if you like. Tilly is very strong."

Humbled again by the fact that she owned so little, Isabelle shook her head.

"I left the food you brought in the cupboards. I hope that's okay. I just packed a snack in case the journey was long."

Bear stopped and the expression on his face was one of compassion. "You did exactly right, milady. We can always replace the supplies. What we cannot ever replace is you."

Touched by his gruff words, she followed him over to where Tilly waited just behind the house. She watched mutely, worry making her shake as Bear attached her bags to the harness that wrapped discretely around Tildeth's chest and back. It was made of pale leather that had been dyed to match the dragoness's coloring, much like Bear's gear, which is probably why she hadn't noticed it before.

Looking back at her house and newly repaired barn, she saw the pile of wood Robert and Growloranth had created for her only a few hours ago. She had been looking forward to a comfortable winter with no need to ration herself on firewood, and now, just a short time later, she was worrying about whether or not her home would still be standing on the morrow.

She didn't realize she was crying until strong arms wrapped around her gently from behind. She was turned into a strong chest, covered in dark fabric. Robert. The dark twin to Bear's sky blue raiment.

"It'll be all right, sweetheart. I promise. No matter what happens in the coming days, you will always have a place at the Lair. You will be welcome there. You'll see." He stroked her hair as he spoke. "We'll watch over your home. No one from the village will molest your homestead, but if skiths come, this is no place for you, sweetheart. We need you to be safe. I could not bear it if you were hurt." His whispered words helped calm her, though the fear wouldn't leave her.

Battle was imminent. People would be hurt and might even die. Skiths were probably going to destroy much of the village, and perhaps the only true home she had ever known. But while Robert held her in his arms, she felt stronger, as if what he hoped would truly come to pass and everything would work out all right.

Hugging him, she sent a prayer up to the Mother of All for his safety. He was such a special man. She hadn't known him long, but she admired him greatly. He was strong and loyal. He'd done so much to see to her comfort already. He was facing untold danger in the coming hours and yet he spared a few minutes to offer her comfort.

"You're being so nice to me," she whispered, rubbing her fingers over his chest as she snuggled into his embrace.

"You're easy to be nice to," he countered. She could hear the smile in his deep voice, and she felt the kiss he placed on the top of her head. "Now, go with Bear and settle in safely at the Lair. I'll be back there tomorrow morning."

She drew back from him and looked up into his eyes. "You're not coming with us?"

"Sweetheart, it's almost dark. That's when Growly and I do our best work." His smile was a little mischievous, which didn't really reassure her. "We have to stay here and see if we can learn more about the enemy's plans."

When she realized he would not be dissuaded, she made a decision. "Mrs. Nethins. The cook at Cleef Mantell's place. She is no friend of her master. If you tell her I sent you, she will talk to you and tell you all you want to know." Isabelle reached up to undo the catch on the only necklace she owned. It had been her mother's and she wore it at all times. "Show her this." Isabelle put the necklace, which consisted of a small silver medallion on a fine chain that was much stronger than it looked, around Robert's neck. "It was my mother's and Mrs. Nethins was a good friend to her, and to me. Warn her about the attack, if you can. She does a final check of Mantell's chicken coop right after dinner."

"I cannot take your mother's charm," Robert protested.

"You must. Mrs. Nethins will not speak freely to you without some sign that you truly are my friend. She knows I would never give this to anyone if it was not the most dire emergency." Isabelle patted the silver charm as it lay on his chest.

Robert covered her hand with his and she looked up into his eyes. "Thank you, Isabelle. I will deliver it back safe to you on the morrow."

64

"See that you do," she said, her throat tightening with emotion.

She worried for his safety with skiths and enemy soldiers ready to pounce. She stood on tiptoe to kiss him and was gratified when he met her halfway, taking her lips with a ferocity that spoke of emotions he didn't seem inclined to discuss outright. That was all right. She understood.

At length, he let her go and set her away from him as if it pained him to do so. She knew how he felt. She didn't want to leave him, even though she knew she must.

"Now be safe and hang on to Bear. Growly and I will be back at the Lair tomorrow morning. I promise you."

"I will hold you to that promise," she tried to be brave and smile, but tears choked her. "Be careful, Robert."

"I will. You too. Follow Bear's instructions and you'll be fine. Tilly has never dropped a novice yet."

"Dropped?" Shocked out of her tears, her mouth dropped open.

"Nice going, Robert," Bear growled, coming up behind her. "Don't frighten the lass. Tilly and I will take good care of you, Isabelle. You will be as safe with us as you are on the ground. Safer—considering there are skiths about. Now come along. We must make our report and mobilize the Lair."

Bear took her hand, leading her toward the waiting dragons. Robert followed behind, keeping close. The knights surrounding her made her feel safer than she had ever felt. Even knowing there were skiths ready to attack her home, having Robert and Bear near made her feel as if nothing could harm her. But the knowledge of the skiths massing nearby made her worry for the knights.

Growloranth and Tildeth had moved through the forest a ways to the small clearing near the river. Isabelle supposed that was so Tildeth would have a clear shot to the sky. Still, Isabelle eyed the opening in the trees doubtfully. She just didn't see how the dragon could make such a steep ascent.

Bear led her right up to Tildeth and stopped. Mindful of

her manners, Isabelle greeted the female dragon with a bow.

"Thank you for agreeing to carry me, Lady Tildeth," Isabelle said to the dragon.

"You are very welcome, child, but come now, there is no time to waste. We must warn the Lair."

Bear instructed her how to climb up to Tildeth's back, using the dragoness's foreleg and knee as a sort of staircase. Tildeth helpfully sat still and arranged her front arm in a way that allowed Isabelle to ascend easily. Bear climbed up behind her, settling his big, warm body tight against her back as his arms came around her.

With a last look at Robert, Isabelle felt Tildeth gather herself and then…jump. The whoosh of her wings unfurling and catching the wind propelled them into the sky.

The rush of flying was like nothing Isabelle could have imagined. It was amazing!

"You are a natural flyer, Lady Isabelle," Tildeth said into Isabelle's mind, surprising her a bit.

"Oh, Lady Tildeth, this is breathtaking!" Isabelle gushed back.

Tildeth seemed to enjoy Isabelle's enthusiasm. She poured on the speed while Bear held Isabelle close, his arm around her middle. The dragon beneath them kept them warm in a way Isabelle hadn't expected, though the air rushed past her face with almost bruising force. Still, it was the most invigorating experience Isabelle had ever had. She loved every minute of flying with Tildeth and Bear.

It took no time at all, it seemed, before they approached the strangest place Isabelle had ever seen. Built into the side of a cliff, there were massive openings where she could just make out dragons walking around. Light shone in the openings in the cliff, outlining the silhouettes of all within. Even as she watched, two dragons launched themselves off the side of the cliff from one of the topmost openings. Isabelle held her breath as a gorgeous violet dragon dipped low, then started beating her wings, heading straight for them. The darker dragon that was slightly higher on the wind currents followed close behind.

"And there is our greeting party," Tildeth said, her voice a low rumble in Isabelle's mind. *"The pretty purple dragon is Vanna and her mate is Iridned, the big blue coming in from above. A nice combination, aren't they? Their offspring are lovely, and good fliers. They and their knights are good friends to our small family."*

"It will be an honor to meet your friends, Lady Tildeth," Isabelle replied politely, trying not to let on how close to overwhelmed she was by it all.

The new dragons circled around them a few times as they headed for one of the ledges. Isabelle felt a bit conspicuous, conscious of the speculative looks the knights who rode on back of the violet and blue dragons were giving her.

"Hold on now," Tildeth warned as she grabbed for the ledge with her back legs, then landed with a bit of a jolt on her forelegs.

Tildeth knelt down and Bear jumped off, reaching up to help Isabelle down. He was moving fast, hustling now to make his report and mobilize the Lair. Already, there was a great deal of movement on the ledge as dragons and knights began to realize something was amiss. No doubt, Tildeth and Bear were both sending silent communications to those around them.

Vanna and Iridned landed right behind Tildeth, and moved up beside her while Bear removed Isabelle's bags from Tilly's back. Two strange knights looked at her, having climbed down from the two dragons and come over to greet Bear and Tildeth.

"Welcome back, Bear," the knight with the longer hair said as Bear came up beside her, holding her bags. "How can we help?"

"Jovan, this is Lady Isabelle. She will be staying in my suite but I cannot bring her there myself at the moment. Can you make sure she's comfortable? And deliver these bags to my suite as well. Be careful of them. The contents are precious to my lady." Bear handed the two bags to the other knight, then turned to her. "Milady Isabelle, please forgive me. My report must be made with all haste, but I would like to make sure you are comfortable. Will you trust my friend here to see you safely to our suite? I promise you may trust him. He will take good care of you and make certain you are left with someone to talk to." The last was said over her head as he looked at his friend, seeking his agreement.

The man called Jovan nodded and smiled. He was very handsome, but to her eyes, he wasn't as good looking as Robert or Bear. Then again, she was probably prejudiced in their favor. In just a couple of days, she had become duly infatuated with both men. She wasn't sure what that might mean for her future just yet, but she was willing to explore where it might lead. For now.

"I trust your judgment, Sir Bernard," she assured him, finding her courage. These men were knights, chosen by dragons to defend all of Draconia. If they couldn't be trusted, who could?

Bear looked relieved. He dropped a quick kiss on her lips that promised silently of more to come—later. Bear left her alone with Sir Jovan as he and Tildeth went off to make their reports. Sir Jovan led her down into the mountain, through a passageway that was wide and tall enough for two dragons to pass with ease.

"So where did Sir Bear find you, if I may ask," Sir Jovan began conversationally as they walked along the brightly lit paths. There were many shafts high up in the walls that led to the outside allowing for ventilation—because dragons tended to smoke a lot—and probably light during the day.

"I live just outside of Halley's Well. It is a small village between the Valla Pass and the River of Jelan," she told him absently, taking in the lovely carvings in the rock that were half-finished in some spots. Apparently this new Lair was still very much under construction. Or somebody was on a beautification kick.

Sir Jovan's gaze lit with interest when she glanced at him. "That is a very strategic area, though most of our attention has been on the larger villages on the northern side of the river. Apparently Bear spotted something on the less navigable side?"

She didn't see the harm in telling what little she knew to the knight. "Sir Bernard said skiths were being herded toward the pass in front of a grouping of enemy soldiers, and I suspect the village's headman is working with the enemy."

Sir Jovan whistled between his teeth even as his body tensed. "No wonder he came back without Robert and Growly."

"They are still on watch, and I believe they will be scouting tonight. Sir Robert said he would be back here in the morning." She heard the shakiness of her own voice, but apparently her fear for Robert and Growloranth's safety was lost on the other knight. He was probably too preoccupied talking silently with his dragon partner, she realized.

They walked the rest of the way to two very large doors in silence. The doors were plain, but heavy, and made of wood. She could already see the patterns she would love to carve on that blank surface if given a chance. Portraits of Growloranth and Tildeth, their necks entwined. And Robert and Bear, standing on either side. But it was a fanciful thought. She would probably never be given the chance to entertain her little hobby of wood carving on such a grand scale.

Sir Jovan threw open the massive doors that were large enough to let Growloranth and Tildeth pass through. There was a massive sand pit in the center of the open space, with small chambers arranged around it in a circle.

"This is the suite assigned to Growloranth, Tildeth, Robert and Bear," he said, walking a short way into the huge cavern. Both dragons would fit in the large pit of sand, and Isabelle could feel the warmth coming from it.

"What makes it so warm?" she asked, walking inside and looking around in wonder.

"Carefully channeled geothermal energy and a touch of magic," answered a new voice from the open doorway.

Isabelle looked up to find a woman at the door. She was dressed in fine clothing and spoke like an educated person. She seemed a bit older than Isabelle, by more than a few years. The lady smiled and entered, reaching out her hand to Isabelle in greeting.

"Sorry to just pop in. I am Silla, the Lair's healer. I heard of your arrival and thought maybe you could use a new friend to talk to while the men go about their business."

Isabelle took the other woman's hand and was pulled into a loose, welcoming hug. This Silla seemed all that was kind in the world. Then again, she claimed to be a healer, so compassion was probably at the core of her being.

"I am Isabelle," she replied quietly, a bit shy of the fine lady.

"Tilly asked me to come. She says you have some knowledge of healing and thought we might get along," Silla advised.

Her manner was so open and joyful it was hard not to like her. And it was clear she could also talk to dragons if Lady Tildeth had spoken to her. It was also clear that Tilly had taken the time to ask this nice woman to seek out Isabelle so she would not be all alone in this strange new place. Isabelle's heart opened for the female dragon who was so thoughtful. Isabelle would have to find some way to repay Tilly's kindness.

"I know the healing ways my mother taught me of herbs and potions but I would never say I am a real healer. I see to the livestock in the village. The midwife takes care of the women and the barber sees to the men. I only heal animals," Isabelle admitted in a rush, shy of the newcomer.

"If you will excuse me," Sir Jovan cut in, already edging toward the door. "Now that you have the best guide possible, I will be on my way. It was an honor to meet you Lady Isabelle. Truly, Bear and Robert will be the envy of the Lair when word about you gets around." Jovan winked at her and fled, heading back up the passageway at a fast clip. No doubt he had preparations to make if the knights and dragons of this Lair were going into battle.

"Fly safe and good hunting, Sir Jovan," she called after him, sending a prayer heavenward to the Mother of All for his safety. Silla was at her side, her smile fading as she no doubt realized Isabelle knew something of what was happening to mobilize the Lair.

"Tilly didn't give me any details because she was off to the dragon council, but there's trouble coming, isn't there?" Lady Silla asked, concern in her voice.

"I am sorry to say, there is," Isabelle replied, her thoughts turning to Robert, still in harm's way this night.

"Tell me what you know," Silla said urgently, leading Isabelle to the small grouping of chairs and a couch, off to one side. Isabelle noticed that Sir Jovan had deposited her two bags of belongings on the low table in the center of the well-padded chairs.

The women sat as Isabelle began to tell Silla the little that she knew of the situation. By the time she was done, Silla was frowning, but her facial expression made Isabelle think the woman was planning.

"I know you're newly arrived here…" Silla said, standing, "…but if you're not too tired, I could use help preparing the salves and other supplies we might need on the morrow, if you're willing."

Isabelle was glad to be asked. She wanted to be useful. And truth be told, she did *not* want to spend any portion of her night all alone, pacing around the circle of this suite, wringing her hands and worrying.

"I'm not tired at all, Lady Silla," Isabelle replied quickly. "I'd be happy to help in any way I can."

Silla smiled again, though not as brightly as before. "Thank you, Isabelle. This Lair is still very new and there are not too many with basic healing skills here yet. I could use an extra pair of hands both in preparation and in treatment, if and when it comes to that. Tilly said you can bespeak dragons?" Silla asked the question as they left the suite together, the massive doors closing easily behind them.

"I can," Isabelle confirmed. "I didn't know it was such a rare thing until Robert and Growloranth told me. I used to speak to my mother the same way, but she was the only one.

I never knew how dragons communicated with their knights until a few days ago."

They walked down a long hall, in a different direction than Jovan had brought her, stopping finally in front of a small, person-sized door. Silla pushed it open and the lovely scent of herbs wafted out to Isabelle even before the door was fully open.

"This is my workroom," Silla told her. "We are close to the cliff face here and there is a hothouse my mates built for my plants just through there." She nodded toward a small, shadowy passage that must lead to the outer wall. "We will concentrate on preparing burnjelly since the first wave will be skiths. Have you used it before?"

Isabelle had to shake her head. "I have heard of it, but nobody in our village has had a plant in more than twenty years, or so the story goes. But if you show me what to do, I'm a quick study. My mother and I spent many hours making salves and ointments from the herbs we gathered in the woods."

They spent the next two hours and more harvesting burnjelly from the stock of plants Silla had in her well-organized hothouse. Silla lectured as she worked, teaching Isabelle a great deal she had not known about healing and the use of plants that she had never seen before. Silla also told Isabelle of her origins and how she had been married at a very young age to an old man in a faraway land. When the old man tired of her, she was beaten to within an inch of her life and thrown out in the gutter to die. Someone took pity on her and brought her to a temple of healing, where she was slowly nursed back to health.

With nowhere to go and a demonstrated aptitude for gardening and preparing herbal remedies, Silla was allowed to stay on at the temple as a student. Eventually she was sent out on her journeyman trial—a trip that usually lasted about ten years, where Temple healers were expected to make their own way in the world, using the skills they had learned and healing all who asked it of them, be it man or beast.

It was at that point that Isabelle realized Silla was a Temple healer. Even in Halley's Well, the skills of those trained in the Temple were well known, even revered. Isabelle had only ever seen one Temple healer come through the village, when she was just a small girl. The healer had taken tea with her mother and they had spoken of different treatments and herbs for several hours.

When the Temple healer left Halley's Well, he had a stock of her mother's seedlings in his cart and Mama had a drawer full of prepared salves and a few new recipes. The villagers hadn't known the Temple healer had spent his last hours in the area having tea with her mother while Isabelle played on with her doll under the table. Even at that young age, Isabelle had learned that the less the villagers knew of their doings, the better.

Silla went on to tell of how she had healed a dragon and fallen in love with his knight, and the knight who was partnered with the dragon's mate. In short order she had wed the two knights and been installed as the new Lair's first healer.

There was so much Isabelle wanted to ask but the night was growing very late and Sir Bernard arrived at the door unexpectedly, to collect Isabelle from Silla's care. They had gotten a huge supply of burnjelly ready. It would steep for the next day or so, becoming even more potent, and ready for when it might be needed.

Bear thanked Silla for looking after Isabelle, and seemed gratified to find that Isabelle had helped out so greatly in the preparations. He seemed…proud…of her, much to Isabelle's surprise and delight. It had been so long since anyone thought anything about her actions. It was a nice feeling that he cared how she got on with the Lair folk.

Sir Bernard escorted her back to the suite where Lady Tildeth was already ensconced in the huge oval sand pit. Her wings were folded, her neck curved back on her body and little tendrils of cinnamon-scented smoke rose softly from her nostrils as she slept.

They slipped quietly around the sand pit and Bear motioned for her to join him in a side chamber that served as a kitchen. He poured two cups of steaming liquid into waiting mugs and offered her one as they sat at a plain wooden table. Isabelle was pleased to find he had brewed an herbal tea that was both soothing and delicious.

"I figured we could use a few minutes to unwind. It has been rather tense since we took to the sky," Sir Bernard said, touching her with his thoughtfulness. "Did you get on well with Lady Silla?"

"She is wonderful," Isabelle told him with candor. "She taught me a great deal and I was able to help her preparations. She invited me back tomorrow, in fact."

"I'm glad. Silla is a highly skilled healer and one of the favorites among every dragon in the Lair."

"Is Lady Tildeth all right?" Isabelle looked out the doorway into the center of the suite and the sandpit where the dragon lay sleeping.

"She's fine. Just very tired. She flew double time to get us here so quickly," he explained. "We could sit outside in the more comfortable chairs. Some nights I sit out there for hours and just watch her, thanking my lucky stars that she chose me as her knight."

Isabelle was fascinated by the dragons. "If you're sure she doesn't mind," she said, rising to follow him out of the kitchen.

"She doesn't," he assured her in a quiet voice. "I asked her. She knows I'm dopey in love with her. I have been for years. She's like mother, sister and best friend, all rolled into one—though there's so much more that I can't describe to our relationship. She is part of me, I guess." He shrugged, seeming at a loss for words. "All I can say is, the day she chose me was the happiest day of my life." He led Isabelle over to the seating area. "As long as we keep our voices down, she'll sleep like a baby."

CHAPTER SIX

They relocated to the much more comfortable, overstuffed chairs and couch arrangement out by the dragon's sand pit, which Isabelle had learned was called a wallow. Isabelle felt the tensions of the day leaving her as she held her steaming mug of tea and sipped at the fragrant brew. She discovered Bear was a peaceful sort of person to be around. She was surprisingly comfortable with him. And she liked the way he spoke of his dragon partner.

"The bond runs deep between a knight and his dragon, doesn't it?" she asked quietly, still very curious about the relationship.

"It is a joining of souls. When Tilly spoke the words of Claim to me and I accepted, something deep inside my being joined with her in a way that is hard to describe. We became part of each other—just a little bit. And I suppose that bond will last until I die, though the very nature of the bond has extended my life beyond the normal number of years. Of course, a dragon knight's life is one of duty, service and occasional violence, so only the Mother of All knows how long I may live."

Isabelle kept silent for a while as they both contemplated his words. The mood was lazy, peaceful, almost intimate. She hadn't shared such moments with anyone before and she found she was enjoying herself very much, even if the rigors of her long day were catching up with her. She smothered another yawn as they sat there, watching the dragon sleep. She truly was a magnificent creature, even in repose.

"You're a lucky man to have Tildeth in your life," Isabelle whispered.

"You'll get no argument from me," he answered after a slight pause.

It was clear they were both tired, but she was too comfortable to move. Isabelle rested her head against the soft leather of the chair and the next thing she knew, she was being lifted in Bear's strong arms. She had fallen asleep.

"I can walk," she said softly, still mostly asleep. Truth to tell, she was exhausted.

"I like taking care of you," Bear admitted, his soft words touching her heart. "Let me."

She rested her head on his shoulder as he walked with her in his arms toward one of the rooms arrayed around the sand pit. Her eyes closed and only opened again when he lowered her to a soft bed. But she didn't want to let him go.

Isabelle kept her hands around his neck as he dipped lower, releasing her body but closing the gap between her lips and his. And then he kissed her.

And she was lost.

She wasn't sure exactly how it happened, but he followed her down onto the bed and lay over her, like a warm, living blanket. He kept most of his weight off her, propping himself up on his forearms. That caused his biceps to flex in the most intriguing way. She couldn't resist running her hands down his shoulders and over his arms. He was so strong. So masculine. So caring on every level.

"I want to make love with you, Isabelle," his voice rasped near her ear, sending delighted shivers down her spine.

She had never been with a man before, but she knew how things worked. One didn't spend much time tending to the health of farm animals without learning the mechanics of sex. She hadn't expected a man's touch to bring such incredible sensations though. She wanted to learn more. Truth be told, she wanted to know it all. She was through with waiting for her life as a woman to begin. There was no princely farmer to sweep her off her feet and make her life one of ease. She had given up those dreams a long time ago.

But here was a new dream. A knight—two of them, if she truly believed what they had been saying, though she still found it hard to imagine that they would both want her for keeps. Still, she would never have a better chance to learn what it was to make love, nor a better man to teach her. Although Robert would have been equally as desirable—which was a thought that gave her serious pause. Could she really be considering the triad relationship they wanted? It still seemed preposterous that they could actually want that...with her, of all people...but the more Bear touched her, the less she could think.

All she knew was, she wanted to finally know what it was to have a man take her body and make her feel more of these incredible sensations. She lifted her hands back up to his face, cupping his cheeks and looking deep into his lovely blue eyes.

"I want you too, Bernard. Show me what it's like. Make me yours," she whispered, unsure where all the courage was coming from, but willing to let it lead her. She liked the direction it was taking her.

Her words seemed to spark something within his gaze. She swore she could almost see flames licking at the blue irises of his eyes. Magical, mystical heat, generated by the two of them...together.

"I will take care with you, my heart. I promise you." He lowered his lips to her mouth, but soon followed a path of his own making down over her chin, to the sensitive spots on her neck and lower...

Somehow her clothing came loose and then disappeared. She was too overwhelmed by sensation to really know how he did it. Perhaps some magic—or just skilled fingers with well-worn laces. Either way, she was drunk on the feeling of skin on skin. That's when she realized his clothing was disappearing too, until he lay over her, his body touching hers from head to toe—and a lot of really interesting places in between.

His lips rubbed over her breasts, exciting them into peaks which she laved with his tongue. She hadn't known men did that to women and she wanted more. The feeling was delicious and caused a serious flutter in her midsection.

She heard a little moan and self-consciously realized it came from her. Bear looked up at her and the grin on his face made her even more self-conscious. She felt heat rise to her cheeks, and his expression changed.

He rose above her, placing one hand on her cheek as he balanced over her. "Do not worry. Nothing we do together is wrong. If I do something you don't like, all you need to do is tell me and I'll stop. If you make a sexy little sound like the one that just escaped, I'll take it as encouragement to do more of the same. Do not censor your responses to my touch, little one. I like to hear your approval of my efforts." His grin returned. "And in a little while, if I continue to be blessed by your approval, you'll hear my sounds of pleasure as well."

He caressed her cheek, then bent over her to kiss her lips, lingering for a long time while she forgot exactly what it was she'd been embarrassed about earlier. Bear had a way of making her forget her own name when he kissed her. Or touched her. Or played with her body in ways that should make her blush, but only elicited more of those little sounds she had no idea she would make at such a time.

Her breathing grew labored as his hands found her most secret places. He rubbed a spot between her legs that made her squirm and when his finger slipped inside her body, she couldn't help the squeak of surprise that came out of her mouth.

It didn't feel anything like she expected. It was strange, and exciting. She realized he was watching her reaction, gauging something only he knew to look for. Her breath hitched as he touched some secret spot inside her, rubbing as he moved his finger back and forth, in and out.

She gripped his arms as her body quaked and the most incredible pleasure washed over her for the first time ever. It was amazing.

"There is more to come," Bear said, his face dipping close to hers to steal another kiss. "I promise you. I will be gentle, but it may hurt at first, since you are new to this."

Isabelle nodded. She knew about the barrier that proved a woman's innocence. She also knew there was no gentler or better man to rid her of it. Bear had already shown her more care and compassion than any other man she had ever known...except for Robert, of course. They were both so kind and so handsome.

Thinking about Robert when she was naked in Bear's arms didn't seem wrong, though her mind did ask the question as to why it seemed so natural. Apparently something inside her saw them as a pair. With one, came the other. They were a matched set—matched by the mating of their dragon partners. This time alone with Bear was the anomaly rather than the norm.

But all in all, it was probably better to deal with only one of them while still carrying the burden of her virginity. One was intoxicating enough. Both of them would have been completely overwhelming.

Bear kissed her again, deeply. He made her squirm with his kiss and with his hand, preparing the way for another part of him that was much bigger than his finger. She hadn't yet seen him, she realized, but she could definitely feel that part of him as it touched her entrance. He was wide, but her body had provided enough lubrication for him to slip inside a short way.

He paused and she felt stretched, but she wasn't in any pain. She was dying of anticipation. She wanted more. Using her hands on his shoulders, she silently urged him to go deeper.

And then he did.

Everything stood still for a moment as a white-hot fire enveloped her lower body. Goddess, that hurt! But Bear didn't move, for which she was eminently thankful. His arms trembled beneath her fierce grip as much as her body did as it tried to assimilate the pain and pleasure, all mixed up in one confusing ball of need.

She wanted...something. To ask him to go? To beg him to stay? She wasn't sure.

But then he took all thought from her mind by moving. The fire of the pain was still there, but it was tempered now with a wash of pleasure that stole her breath. Each small movement of his body brought conflicting waves of agonizing pleasure. She wasn't sure she could survive whatever was coming, but she felt something building. Something immense and unfathomable.

She wanted to know. She wanted to feel whatever it was. To experience all that Bear had to offer her that night. Her pleasure was like a series of rippling waves lapping at the riverbank, each one a tiny bit bigger than the last. The sensations built and soon she was gasping as he moved over her, in her, with her.

And then the wave broke and she cried out as an even higher peak of pleasure rippled through her body, taking Bear with it. She heard his groan meld with her higher pitched sounds as he came within her. The warmth of his body over her, inside her, drowned her in the pleasure of their closeness.

She breathed in his musky scent, memorizing everything about him, loving this moment. As first times went, she was certain this was one unlike any other. Bear had hurt her, yes. That was unavoidable. But he'd more than made up for it with the pleasure that followed.

He rolled away from her, taking his body from hers, and she almost reached to pull him back, but she should have known he wouldn't dismiss her so easily. He rolled, pulling her into his arms from behind, spooning with her and pulling the blanket over them both. He placed a tender kiss on her temple and within moments, the pleasure and the length of her day caught up with her, pulling her into a satisfied sleep in the arms of her lover.

Bear woke her the next day before dawn. He kissed her awake and though she would have liked to make love to him again, he put her gently away from him when she would have taken the kiss deeper.

"I'm sorry, my love. We must go out on patrol. Tilly and I are about to leave, but I didn't want to part without saying goodbye. I'll be back later today. Probably after dark, unless I'm needed here before then. But Robert and Growloranth will be along in a few hours. They'll have reports to make, of course, but you will see them today."

"I've warmed a bath for you," Tildeth said into her mind. *"It will stay warm for a while, but you might want to use it sooner rather than later. Or my mate can rewarm it for you after he returns."* Isabelle looked past Bear's shoulder to realize Tilly had craned her neck over to look into the open archway of the bedchamber. Even as Isabelle looked at her, the dragon winked one blue eye at her. *"I am happy you and Bear are getting along so well. He is a good man, is he not?"*

Isabelle could only nod as she realized the dragon was well aware that Isabelle and Bear had had sex last night. And the dragon apparently approved.

"Thank you for preparing the bath," Isabelle said to both of them. She wasn't going to acknowledge the veiled reference to having sex. She wasn't *that* comfortable with her newfound sexuality yet. After all, only a few hours ago, she'd been a virgin. This new state would take some getting used to.

"It was our pleasure," Bear said, dipping low to kiss her again. "And now, we really must go. I'm sorry. I wish it were otherwise, but we have our duty. We'll be with you again as soon as we may."

"I understand," Isabelle said, scrambling for her dignity. She wished he could stay too, but she knew there were many more people counting on him. He and Tilly were probably the only ones who could scout enemy skies without being seen. Their information could save many lives. She smiled for him. "Fly safe and be careful," she said to both of them.

"Good hunting."

Bear smiled brightly at her. Apparently she'd said the right thing. He left the bedroom with one last look for her and then she heard him opening the massive wooden doors and the swish of sand as Lady Tildeth left her wallow. The big doors closed behind them and Isabelle flopped down on the bed when she realized she was alone.

Then she bounced right back up after realizing she was sore. Really sore. The hot bath Tilly had promised sounded really good right about now, and the water wasn't going to get any hotter. Isabelle crawled out of bed, only then realizing the white linens had been smeared with blood. Her blood.

Hands on hips, Isabelle decided to deal with one thing at a time. First order of business was the bath. Then she would see about changing the sheets.

Lady Silla came to get her for breakfast a few hours later, after she'd had that lovely bath in a sunken tub that was more like a small pool. It had steps down into it and it was lined with mosaic tiles in a beautiful pattern of twining dragons in flight. It was more a work of art than a bathing tub.

It was as pretty as it was luxurious. And Tilly had left the water nice and hot for Isabelle. That, plus the bath salts Bear must have mixed into the water, went a long way toward soothing her sore muscles, though the ache between her thighs reminded her of what they had done only a few hours before.

She had spent a long time in the bath, during which the sun had risen and natural light filtered down into the suite through dozens of small ventilation shafts. Having the dragons in here meant there was a need to vent their scented smoke, and the shafts seemed to do that while also allowing daylight to enter the heart of almost every chamber in the suite.

Isabelle had gone exploring, finding a few storage areas— one for what looked like spare bits of armor and tack for the dragons, one that held cleaning supplies, including several brooms, and one that had clothes in need of repair as well as a stack of clean sheets and towels. She took a fresh set of sheets and made up Bear's bed, leaving the stained ones to soak in a small tub she had found in the linen chamber and brought into the bathing room. She filled it with cold water from the ingenious tap system along the far wall, and dipped the stained parts of the sheet in to soak.

She was just starting to search through the small kitchen chamber for anything she could put together for breakfast when a knock sounded on the massive doors. A moment later, she found herself in Silla's company, being whisked through the massive corridors toward a great hall.

Silla told her how the great hall was used for assembling the entire Lair when events were held, but otherwise it served as a communal dining hall that served breakfast, lunch, dinner and snacks for those on odd rotations. Silla told her—and she could still hardly believe it—that Isabelle was welcome to replenish the small kitchen in the suite with any of the many foods found in the great hall. All she had to do was ask one of the people running the buffet and a basket would be packed for her to take back to her suite.

They were halfway through a delicious breakfast of eggs and fresh fruit when Robert walked in. Seeing him, she rose to her feet almost unconsciously and he started toward her. She found herself moving too and they met in the aisle, coming together in a huge hug of welcome.

"I'm so relieved to see you," she blurted out. His leathers were still cold from the outdoors. He had to have come directly here, looking for her, after he landed. She stepped back, realizing everybody was looking at them. "Is Sir Growloranth well?"

Robert let her go, a slight grin on his face. "Growly's fine. How are you settling in, sweetheart? Do you like it here?"

He seemed truly concerned for her comfort, which touched her deeply. "It's amazing here," she answered candidly. "Lady Silla has been all that is kind." She motioned back to the table where she had been sitting with the other woman. Silla was smiling at them and waved at Robert in greeting.

He escorted Isabelle back to the table. "Thank you, Lady Silla, for helping Isabelle learn where things are," he said formally. Silla waived away his thanks with a smile.

"It is my pleasure. Your lady was very helpful to me, helping prepare the medicines we may need for the coming difficulties."

Robert's expression turned into a pensive frown. "My apologies, ladies, I need to make my report, but I think Isabelle should come with me. She needs to hear what I've learned and she also needs to help explain her village to our leaders. Can you do that, Isabelle?" He reached for her hand, looking deep into her eyes.

When he looked at her like that, she could deny him nothing. And truly, she wanted to help these knights. She wanted to help, in whatever small way she could, to defend Draconia, her adopted homeland. Even though she was nervous about meeting important people, she would gather her courage and do what she could. She nodded at Robert.

"Whatever I can do to help, I will." Robert's smile broadened and he squeezed her hands.

"Great. Let's go before they send the dragons after me. So far, Growloranth's been holding them off, but they're going to be huffy that I made them wait." He dipped his head and placed a quick kiss on her lips. "I just had to see my lady first. The rest of the world can wait a few minutes, can't they?"

A dragon trumpeted near the door, drawing his attention.

"Hmm," he muttered. "Apparently not. Let's go."

He led her by the hand out of the great hall, amused glances following their every move. They left the great hall and ran straight into Growloranth and another dragon who was tapping his foreleg in a clear show of impatience. Isabelle had to fight not to grin. For such magnificent creatures, it was kind of funny to see them imitating such an altogether human action.

"It is good to see you again, Sir Growloranth," Isabelle

said, remembering her manners and bowing to the male dragon she knew.

Growloranth nodded his massive head and made the introductions. *"This impatient youngster is Kelvan, partner to Sir Gareth, mate to Princess Belora,"* he said into their minds.

Princess? That word gave her pause. This dragon was kin to powerful folk. Isabelle bowed, giving him all due respect. "It is an honor to meet you, Sir Kelvan."

The blue-green dragon cocked his head, as if he was surprised to be addressed by name. Had she made a mistake? She fidgeted as she straightened, nervous.

"Then you do hear us when we speak." Sir Kelvan asked, moving close to peer into her eyes.

"Yes, sir. I do," she answered in kind, since his objection seemed to be over the extent of her abilities to hear and speak mind-to-mind. His great head jerked back and a tendril of startled smoke rose from his snout.

The younger dragon seemed to backtrack. *"You are most welcome in the Lair, Lady Isabelle. Sir Growloranth has spoken well of you. I hope you will not mind speaking with our council. There is much to discuss and little time to delay."*

The younger dragon was back to being impatient again and Isabelle merely followed behind when he turned to walk quickly in a direction she had not gone before. They were moving up the mountain, if the slope of the corridor they were in was anything to go by. Up they went, Robert and Growloranth at her side while the impatient Kelvan led the way, until finally they arrived at a massive chamber near the top of the mountain that already held three other dragons and several sets of knights. And surprisingly, at least two other women.

Robert walked with her to a central table around which the humans stood. They began to take their seats when Robert and Isabelle arrived and the dragons arranged themselves around the sides of the big chamber.

"Isabelle, this is General Jared, his fighting partner, Lord Darian, their mate, Princess Adora and their dragon partners,

Lady Kelzy and Sir Sandor." Isabelle scrambled to keep the names and faces straight. Kelzy was the same blue-green as the impatient male dragon who had escorted him, while her mate was a dark bronze-brown. The two men were older, as was their lady—the princess. Lord Darian was handsome in a rakish sort of way, and the General had a long scar down one cheek. They would be easy to remember.

She nodded politely, curtseying as her mother had taught her, to all the humans, and bowing to the dragons. Robert then turned her attention to the younger grouping.

"You've already met Sir Kelvan. He partners Sir Gareth and is Lady Kelzy and Sir Sandor's son, as you probably can see from the resemblance. He is mated to the lovely Lady Rohtina, who partners Sir Lars, and his mate is the Princess Belora, who is Princess Adora's youngest daughter."

It was confusing to follow, but Isabelle sorted out the knights by matching them to their dragons and the princess was a younger version of her mother. Both women were very beautiful and had kind expressions on their faces. Isabelle greeted them all with due respect.

"The other knights are Sir Broderick and Sir Geoff, mated to your new friend, Lady Silla. Their dragons are acting as go-betweens for the Dragon Council which is being held above, on the summit of the mountain, which is why they are not here with us. Everyone in this chamber and in the Dragon Council will hear what transpires here this morning."

Isabelle nodded to the two knights and tried to picture them with Silla. It seemed Silla had found two very handsome men to be her life partners.

The idea that all the dragons above—however many were part of their council—and everyone here would possibly be asking her questions and listening to her words was daunting. Isabelle had never had much interaction with large groups of people, and certainly not people or dragons of this kind of pedigree. She was nervous.

"I'm right here," Robert sent directly to her mind, privately, as he squeezed her hand. *"You have nothing to fear."*

She prayed he was right. This gathering was beyond intimidating.

"Sir Robert, please start with your observations," General Jared commanded, sitting forward in his chair as Robert seated Isabelle, then took the chair at her side. "Sir Growloranth, please add your observations as well. We need to know exactly what we're up against." The general spoke to Growloranth in a way that made Isabelle respect the man. He treated dragons as equals and partners, which she should have expected, seeing as he was a knight.

But he was also in a position of power and she always half-expected those in authority to abuse it in some way. After all, that's the behavior she had seen in her own village up to this point. Maybe, just maybe, that was all about to change.

"The news is troubling, my lords," Robert began. "Growloranth and I prowled the village of Halley's Well last night and there is much amiss there. The village headman, a miscreant named Cleef Mantell, is colluding with the enemy. There is no doubt about it. Before my very eyes, he was given a sign to put over his door by an enemy agent so that the invading troops would know to leave his place—as well as any other home that carried the sign—alone, when they arrived. The enemy agent stated quite plainly that anyone who fought would be killed. By promising not to fight, the headman is basically giving ground to the enemy. He is a traitor of the worst kind."

Isabelle wasn't all that shocked, though she couldn't imagine the audacity of Cleef to turn traitor in such a distinct way. He always liked to hedge his bets, timing things so that he came out on top. She wouldn't be surprised if he had some way to deny his involvement ready, in case things went wrong.

"How did you procure this information?" Lord Darian asked.

"On the advice of Lady Isabelle, I made contact with the cook in Mantell's household. She is loyal to the crown. She let me in the back door and arranged for me to hide in an adjacent room while Mantell entertained his foreign visitor. I saw it all with my own eyes."

"There can be no doubt then," Princess Adora said. "This Cleef Mantell must be dealt with and the invasion stopped. If the enemy gets a foothold on this side of the border—particularly in Halley's Well—they could well take every border village up and down the line, moving unseen under the forest canopy. From there, they could attack this Lair and the larger towns and cities. They could become deeply entrenched on this side of the mountains and claim large swaths of Draconia for Skithdron. That cannot be allowed to happen." A grim silence met her words as they all thought of such eventualities for a moment. Then the younger princess turned to Isabelle.

"What can you tell us of the village itself, Isabelle?" Princess Belora asked gently.

"It is a village like any other," Isabelle began, but she soon realized these people needed details that could help their plans. She cleared her throat and tried again. "Cleef Mantell is a snake. He has set up his mansion on the edge of the village under careful cover of the trees. He does not want his growing empire seen from above. He also keeps a low profile when strangers come to the village, except when playing the poor, ignorant farmer. In truth, he is anything but ignorant. He has an extensive library and reads and writes. He also speaks other tongues. My mother said he spoke the language of Talinor. She knew it from her travels, and recognized it when he slipped into what she thought was his mother tongue when he spoke with his wife."

"Talinor is a kingdom across the sea from Helios," Sir Sandor said, his voice reaching them all. *"In the last briefing from Prince Hugh, he stated his belief that the assassins called* Eyes *were from that land."*

"Eyes?" Isabelle was startled into speaking. "Cleef Mantell has an eye-shaped tattoo on his chest, right in the center." She pointed to her own sternum. "It was the talk of the village several seasons ago when his shirt ripped open during harvest. Everyone saw it and several dared to remark on it to him. He said he'd gotten very drunk one night when he visited the city of Tipolir and woke up with it. Claimed some tart had made off with his coin and left him only a weird tattoo to remember her by. He also claimed to be from the south, near Tipolir, but my mother always thought he was lying about that. She stayed far away from Cleef Mantell and counseled me to do the same."

"It sounds like your mother was a wise woman," Kelzy offered. *"Growloranth tells me she is no longer with us—my condolences—and that Tildeth believes she carried the blood of the Fair Folk."* Kelzy's large head loomed over the table, her jewel-like eyes looking directly at Isabelle. *"You have the scent of their magic about you, though it is faint. And you can bespeak dragons, which argues in favor of you carrying a small trace of their magic. Do you know where your mother came from? I understand you were not born in Draconia."*

"My mother came here from over the northern border. She chose this land because she thought I would be safe here. She also said my future was here. Sometimes she had visions of the future and when she foresaw my destiny was in Draconia, she decided to give up the life of a traveling bard and settle here. I was very small, but I remember her singing to large crowds of people when I was little. She was celebrated—or maybe that's just my memories. She often joined with groups of other bards and played with them. I remember brightly painted wagons and dark haired people who were always smiling and played the most beautiful music."

"The Jinn?" Lord Darian theorized. "Maybe we should contact Prince Nico or see if Sir Drake is anywhere near."

"I remember a young man named Drake," Isabelle volunteered. "He had a strong voice and the people we traveled with were teaching him. He was golden blonde and could play many instruments."

"That sounds like our Drake," Jared said with a grin. "I think we had best send him a message. He may be able to tell us more about your mother," he said, not unkindly. "But for now, we must concentrate on the village and its traitorous headman.

What followed was some of the most intense questioning of Isabelle's life. They wanted to know the layout of the village, which she, Growloranth and Robert supplied. They wanted to know who lived in each house and what their jobs were in the village, also if they were likely to side with Mantell. Isabelle answered each question as best she could and was amazed by the drawing Princess Belora made on a large parchment laid before her on the table. It was an exact map of the village, with notations stating who lived where and what they did.

Isabelle was glad her mother had taught her to read and write, so she did not look quite so ignorant in front of these important people. She sent up a prayer of thanks to the Mother of All and her own mother, who had brought her here to these good people, able to help defend the land that she had been raised in and had come to love.

When the meeting finally broke up, Robert escorted Isabelle back to the great hall where lunch was being served. They dined together and she was amazed by the wide selection of foods that were available. Robert explained that dragons routinely flew between Lairs and often brought supplies in from other parts of the country.

"By the way..." Robert said, reaching into his shirt to withdraw the chain he still wore about his neck, "...I promised to return this to you." He removed the necklace and handed it back to her. "It worked just as you said. Mrs. Nethins would not speak to me until I showed her the pendant. And then she insisted on questioning me to within an inch of my life about your wellbeing. Finally, I had to point out where Growly was hiding before she would believe who and what I was. After that, she cooperated. She sends her good wishes, by the way. And she said you should never forget where you came from, whatever that means. She made me promise to repeat it exactly like that."

Isabelle took the necklace and put it back on. She had felt it missing these past hours, but knew Robert would keep it safe. She trusted him as she had trusted no one since her mother had died.

"Thank you. I'm sorry she gave you a hard time, but she is a good woman. I knew she would help you if she knew she could trust you."

"You were right about that, milady. I could not have gotten the evidence we truly needed without her help."

He changed the subject and they talked of less worrying things while they ate. Robert greeted a few people who passed their table. It was easy to see that he was popular among his contemporaries. She wasn't surprised. He was a very nice man, in addition to being incredibly charming.

As they left the great hall, Growloranth caught Isabelle's attention, chatting about their suite and asking if she liked it. She was conversing with the dragon when Silla approached. Distracted by the dragon, Isabelle saw the healer slip something to Robert, which he tucked into his pocket. She thought little of it until they arrived back at his suite.

CHAPTER SEVEN

"I have it on good authority that you might be a little sore today," Robert announced when they arrived back at his quarters. The sand pit was empty and they had the place completely to themselves. "Lady Silla gave me strict instructions on how to treat you."

"Oh, she did? Did she?" Isabelle challenged him in the same playful tone he had used. He stalked her around the oblong circle of the sand pit, but she wasn't scared. Robert was at his most charming and playful. "What did she tell you to do to me?"

The tension that had built between them all through lunch was coming to a head. Isabelle didn't really recognize herself at the moment, but she liked the new freedom she felt to play these new grown-up games with Robert. Or Bear. Or both. It didn't seem to matter. Both men held a rather large chunk of her heart already.

She would have been afraid of her newfound horniness, but her desire was limited to Robert and Bear alone. None of the other knights she had seen had roused any sort of response in her, though many of them were handsome and all were fit specimens of manhood. No, only Robert and Bear flipped her switch and made her want to have her way with them—or have them have their way with her.

Since both men, and their dragons, seemed to think that was perfectly all right, she couldn't really question her response too much. Apparently this was as it should be for knights and their lady.

But was she really going to be their lady? The thought still managed to boggle her mind. She had made love with Bear not really acknowledging the idea that she might be able to live this dream of having them both in her life on a long-term basis. But now Robert seemed to want her. If she let him have her—and she was leaning heavily toward jumping his bones before too much more time had passed—then she might have to consider their proposition more seriously. Maybe this could work. Maybe she could be the woman for these two knights.

Only time would tell. But now she was more open to the possibility that this strange relationship might actually work. She'd seen other triads in the Lair now, and they had all seemed happy. Silla had even discussed her own mating with Isabelle and she thought she understood it all a little better now.

"Come with me, sweetheart, and let me take care of you," Robert said, the teasing replaced by a caring smile that warmed her heart.

Almost without conscious thought, she found her feet moving toward him. He held out a hand and she took it. She let him lead her to a room opposite of the one she had lain with Bear in the night before. The room he chose was also a bedroom, but this one was clearly Robert's. It held mementoes that fit his personality. Gear for Growloranth lay neatly piled in one corner and a polished metal mirror above a chest of drawers sat against another wall. The dominant piece of furniture, just like in Bear's room, was the bed.

He led her to it and they both sat on the side of the wide expanse, side by side, tilted slightly toward each other. Robert kept hold of her hand.

"I know you and Bear were together. He's had all the firsts with you so far and though I love him like a brother, right now I'll admit, I'm jealous as hell." Robert squeezed her fingers. "Will you let me take care of you, sweetheart? I promise we won't do anything you aren't ready for. I just want to touch you and kiss you, and hold you while I sleep. Will you indulge me?"

She was touched by his words. "There's nothing to be jealous of, Robert." She reached up and placed one palm against his cheek, enjoying the sensation of his beard stubble against her skin. "While I might not be up for everything, I promise I'll let you know how far we can go. I'd like to lay with you, even if it's just to cuddle," she admitted. "I am sore, but maybe Silla's medicine will help with that." She lowered her hand from his face and held it out for the small package Silla had slipped to Robert earlier, but he refused to give it up.

"Oh, no, my dear. Lady Silla gave me explicit instructions. It will be my pleasure to act as your doctor in this instance." He winked at her and she felt her cheeks heat. Did he really intend to doctor her injuries *there*?

"Now, my pretty patient," Robert said, rising to his feet and motioning for her to rise as well. "I believe we should start by removing all your clothes." His businesslike tone made her hesitate, then want to giggle after she saw the dancing merriment in his eyes. "Are you shy?" he asked with pretend concern. "Well then, we can't have that. Perhaps it will make you less shy if we both removed our clothes. Then you wouldn't be the only one naked." His teasing made her blush grow deeper, but she was also excited by the idea of being naked with Robert. "How about I remove your dress while you work on my tunic?"

Emboldened by the dare in his gaze, she reached for the hem of his tunic and pulled slowly upward. He stood still, letting her do as she willed. Thankfully, he had rid himself of his sword belt and gauntlets earlier. There was no impediment to her pulling the well-worn fabric up over his head.

And then she got to look at the play of his muscles over his broad chest. He had magnificent shoulders and she found her hands drawn to them, caressing his skin, tracing the faint lines of scars that were a testament to the fact that he was a fighting man.

"Now your turn," Robert said after a moment, his breathing a little faster than it had been before.

He reached down with both hands and gathered the fabric of her dress in his hands, lifting it upward an inch at a time. He moved closer, his hands moving from her sides a little more around her back. His fingers rubbed against her backside and when the hem reached his fingers, he held it with one hand while the other caressed her bare buttocks, rubbing and squeezing.

Then he lifted the dress higher and held the fabric at her back while his other hand rubbed upward, against her ribcage. His fingers teased the undersides of her breasts and she was glad she hadn't had a chance to unpack her bags before he'd come in. She'd simply thrown her dress on after her bath and there were no under things to get in his way.

He held her gaze as his fingers grazed upward, over the peak of one breast. She gasped when he paused, his thumb and forefinger squeezing her nipple. Bear hadn't done that. His touch had been gentler, less demanding, though just as exciting.

"Seems you like that," Robert whispered, moving his hand to her other breast. "How about this?" He rubbed little circles around the tip of her breast, flicking the taut nipple with his fingertip.

Her knees almost gave out and he grinned. Then the dress whooshed up and over her head in one quick move. Before she could even miss him, he was back. Both hands covering her breasts now, squeezing and teasing the tips. He held her gaze as his head lowered and she nearly swooned when his mouth opened over her breast, licking, nipping and then sucking in a way that made her throw her head back and moan.

"Oh yes, you definitely like that." She lifted her head and opened her eyes to find him grinning.

And then he bent, scooped her into his arms, and deposited her on the bed, coming down to rest at her side. He didn't stop kissing her skin, paying special attention to her straining nipples, even as his hands lowered and spread her legs apart. His fingers rubbed delicate circles around the little nubbin at the apex of her thighs, causing her to squirm. She felt the soreness that hadn't quite left her all day and it did temper her reactions a bit.

No way would she be able to take him inside her. Not with the residual pain that made her feel so raw inside. She wanted to, though. She wanted so much to feel his possession as she'd felt Bear's last night. She wanted to know them both in the most intimate way possible.

Robert worked his way down her body and she nearly screamed when his tongue flicked over that little nub between her thighs. Then he was kissing her *there*. It seemed impossible. Unlikely, at best, but he was doing it. Teaching her all new things about her body and what drove her wild.

He moved down on the bed, positioning himself between her spread thighs. He worked at her clit until she came hard against his face and while she was still reeling from the unexpected orgasm, he sat up between her thighs and spread them even wider, placing one of her knees over each of his.

He still wore his pants and he reached into the pocket, removing the small jar Silla had given him. He opened it and the pungent fragrance of rare herbs she recognized hit her. Oh, yes. That would numb the pain and begin the healing nicely. But was Robert really going to administer it? It certainly looked as if that was his plan.

If she wasn't still enjoying a magnificent buzz from the intense pleasure he'd just given her, she might have objected. As it was, she let him do as he willed. She watched, her desire rising again—much to her surprise—as he dipped one long finger into the jar, coating his digit with the salve.

"Now just relax and let Doctor Robert make you all better," he teased, lowering his finger to her core. "Be a good girl and later, I'll give you a treat."

She wanted to giggle at his words, but just then he slipped his finger into her sore passage. Almost immediately the soreness abated. Then other sensations began to take over. The feel of his long finger exploring her recesses, spreading relief and a bit of renewed excitement wherever he touched.

His thumb rose to tease her clit as his finger massaged her passage, spreading the lubrication of the salve and her own juices liberally. She wanted...more. Desire riding her, she wanted to feel him inside her, even if it wasn't the wisest course of action.

"Robert... I want you..." she choked out.

"Well, you can't have me. At least not this way. I'm under strict orders," he replied, making her want to growl in frustration. But something he'd said caught her attention.

"What other way is there?" she asked, curious and wanting.

Robert laughed and the sound held a promise of sensual delight. "There are many ways, sweetheart. Many, many ways. And if you are willing to try something new, I will show you one of them. Do you trust me?"

There was no question in her mind. "Of course I trust you. What sort of question is that?"

Robert laughed at her impatience. "Right, then." He removed his finger from her pussy and sat back. "Flip over," he ordered curtly.

She was confused. She looked at him and he made a little turning motion with one finger, his gaze filled with both encouragement and amusement. She complied, watching him over her shoulder as she presented him with her back.

"Tuck your knees under you and show me that pretty ass of yours." His tone was sinful, making her hesitate, but the promise of pleasure and her trust in him made her comply.

When she was propped up on her folded legs, her butt in the air, his hands returned. The finger that was still coated with salve residue rimmed her back hole, shocking her. And then he pushed inward, making her squeak in surprise. Did he really mean to take her there?

"Relax, sweetheart. Calm down and let me in. I won't hurt you. It'll feel good, I promise, and if you're scared or you don't like it, I'll stop. Just tell me, all right?" His crooning words penetrated her shock and she nodded. She trusted him. He wouldn't hurt her.

She began to relax and then things started to change. Shock turned to pleasure and as she calmed, she began to realize the sensations coming from his actions were strange, but kind of amazing too.

He let her get used to the sensations before adding a finger and stretching her. And then, after she was about ready to beg, he finally moved over her and began to claim her with his body. It was much more intense and she caught her breath as he paused only part-way inside.

"All right, sweetheart?" he asked, his own breathing ragged.

"I'm good. Keep going," she urged. "Just go slow."

He bent over her, placing a kiss on the side of her head. "You're amazing, Isabelle."

She felt amazing as he moved deeper into her. The feeling was so strange, yet oddly pleasurable. She knew she wouldn't like this with anyone other than Robert or maybe Bear, but with the two men who held pieces of her heart, she was willing to try almost anything.

And then Robert began to move. He went slow, as she requested, and gradually built up speed. It was never fast, but it was more than enough to push her over the peak into a hard, fast climax, which took him with her. He pulled out and she felt the splash of his climax pulse over her backside. He gripped her hips with one hand and she looked back to see his other hand wrapped tight around his cock, still spurting against her. She leaned back a bit to rub against him, liking the way he groaned.

That was about all she was good for before collapsing on the bed. Robert followed soon after. She must have dozed for a while, but she woke when Robert placed her into her second hot bath of the day.

Growloranth must have come back at some point while she slept. She could just see him through the open door that led to the wallow. She flushed realizing the dragon must have been witness to Robert carrying her naked body across the length of the suite.

"Are you awake?" Robert asked, his head above hers as he joined her in the bath that was big enough for two—or three.

"Barely, but yes, I'm awake. Thanks for drawing the bath."

"It's the least I could do since I'm the one who made you dirty." His words seemed to have more than one meaning and she turned in his arms to look at his face. Sure enough, he was smiling at her in that wicked way he had.

She leaned in to kiss him and was gratified when he returned her kiss after a slight hesitation. Had she taken him by surprise? Well, good. She needed to have the upper hand in this relationship every once in a while. If they were going to have a relationship.

More and more it seemed that they were. She was beginning to believe that it might just possibly work. She had bedded both men and enjoyed each occasion immensely. She still wasn't sure how the whole mating flight triple bonding would work, but she might give it more serious consideration if things kept going like this.

If Silla and other women in the Lair had such relationships, then maybe Isabelle and her men could make it work too. It was something to think about, at the very least.

For Robert, life couldn't get much better than it was at that very moment. He had the woman of his dreams lying naked in his arms, in a tub full of steaming water. His dragon partner lay nearby, in his own wallow, sleeping the sleep of the righteous. They had put in a good night's work and might just have been able to report things back to their leaders that would save many lives in the coming conflict.

All in all, it had been a good day.

The only thing that would be better is if Isabelle was firmly committed to them. If she was already their wife and he knew she would always be with them, waiting for them when they flew home or working at their sides to make the world a better place. She was such a special woman. He prayed to the Mother of All that she would accept them—and everything that entailed.

Robert yawned loudly, unable to hold it back. It had been a good night, but a long one. He couldn't really remember the last uninterrupted sleep he'd had.

"We should go to bed," Isabelle murmured. He tightened his arms around her.

"I like the sound of that," he agreed, kissing her hair.

"To sleep," she said firmly, though her tone held a hint of humor. "You were up all night and then making reports all morning. I doubt you even had a single solid hour of rest anywhere in there. You need to get some sleep." She gestured toward the doorway and the dragons' wallow beyond. "Your partner has the right idea."

Caught, he had to agree. "Yes." He sighed heavily. "You're right, of course." He moved her forward in the water and sat up, preparing to leave the cooling bath. She gasped when he lifted her in his arms and walked up the steps of the recessed tub, placing her on her feet in the doorway of the chamber.

"A little help, my friend?" Robert spoke in the direction of the snoozing dragon. Growloranth didn't even stir. He simply breathed a little harder in their direction, sending a warming, cinnamon-scented wind over them, drying their bodies within moments.

Robert lifted her in his arms again and carried her into the one chamber in their suite that had been empty since they had moved in. It was the one chamber he had dreamed of having filled—by the right woman. It had a massive bed in the center of the chamber, but no one lived in it. Not yet, at least.

"Where are we?" she asked as he put her down on the bed.

"This is the mates chamber of our suite. It's been empty until now, since we didn't have a mate, but as you can see, it is big enough for the three of us, when needed." He lay down next to her and pulled a thin blanket over both of them.

He pulled her back against him so that they were spooned together. He liked the feel of her in his arms. Within a few moments, even though he had a great deal to think about, they were both fast asleep.

Robert woke a few hours later when he heard the massive door to their suite open and close. Coupled with the sounds of a dragon wading into the sand pit and the slip of scales on scales, and he figured that Bear and Tilly had returned. Finally. The whole family was together in one place.

"We're in the mates chamber, Bear," Robert sent silently to his fighting partner.

"That was fast work," came the dry reply. A moment later Robert heard footsteps and then Bear walked through the open portal. *"Has she agreed to be our mate?"*

"Not quite yet, but I think she's warming to the idea."

Bear sat on the side of the bed, next to Isabelle. The movement of the mattress woke her.

"Bear," she said, still charmingly groggy. "You're back."

Bear dropped down to place a lingering kiss on her lips. "I'm back," he whispered against her mouth, then drew away. "Am I to understand you've been sleeping most of the afternoon?"

"Well, you kept her up most of the night. It hasn't been an easy couple of days for any of us," Robert replied for her, sitting up in the bed and leaning back against the headboard.

"Much as I would enjoy exploring this giant bed with you, my dear..." Bear whispered near her ear as she hid under the blanket, "...my first duty is to be certain you have all that you need. In this case, I believe dinner is in order."

At that moment, her stomach growled delicately and Robert realized Bear was right. They hadn't eaten since lunch and it was already past dinnertime. She had to be hungry. Robert threw off the blanket and launched himself out of the bed, seeking his clothing. Their woman was hungry. They had to fix that right away.

With quite a few blushes, Isabelle was persuaded to get out of bed and get dressed. Within a few minutes more, they were on their way to the great hall. There they collected three dinner trays and sat down at an empty table. The prime dinner hour was already past, so there weren't that many people left in the hall and they had the place mostly to themselves.

Still, the food was hot and filling. Robert saw to it that Isabelle had all she wanted and a few things she had never tried before. He liked showing her new things—even small things like exotic fruits from afar.

"I wonder where everyone is?" Robert mused, looking around the deserted hall. "Even at this hour it is usually more crowded here."

Bear looked chagrined. "Apologies, my friend. I thought you knew, but then how could you if you've been asleep all afternoon? The news from Halley's Well is not good. We saw troops massing and I believe the invasion is set for tomorrow morning. I suspect they will herd the skiths across the pass at first light. Everyone is preparing for battle."

Isabelle gasped, but Robert wasn't all that surprised. He had been expecting action sooner rather than later.

"I assume the other dark dragons will be watching over the village and the pass tonight, then, since we haven't been called," Robert observed.

"You've got that right," Bear confirmed. "Jared and Darian wanted us to fight as a pair on the morrow, which means you've got the night off."

Robert smiled. "I wonder, how ever shall we spend it?"

Isabelle blushed and he knew she was both embarrassed and excited. He loved her innocent reactions to him and looked forward to seeing if she could be with both he and Bear. If that last barrier could be crossed, it would be a major step forward. If she could take them both and enjoy it, she could finally be their mate. It was all up to her, though Robert prayed silently to the Mother of All that Isabelle could be convinced to be their wife. He wanted her with him—with them—forever and always.

Tonight might prove to be vital in his and Bear's campaign to make her theirs.

CHAPTER EIGHT

When they returned to the suite after dinner, Isabelle knew what the men had in mind. Robert's subtle teasing and Bear's molten glances gave away their hopes and excited her senses at the same time. Could she?

Dare she?

Isabelle thought more and more that she would at least like to give it a try. She wasn't sure if she had it in her to be with both of them at the same time, but if she could... If she could...her whole world might change. For the better.

If she could love them both—physically as well as from the heart—then it was becoming clear that they would welcome her into their life. She knew it was up to her, and she was trying really hard not to let fear hold her back from reaching for something she'd thought would be unattainable. Love was within her grasp. She just had to be brave enough to claim it.

The dragons were in their wallow, their necks touching as they lay there resting. Little curlicues of cinnamon-scented smoke wafted toward the vents in the ceiling, and heat from the dragons made the entire suite warm. It was a homey atmosphere. Especially when Bear went into the kitchen and came out with three steaming mugs of tea on a tray.

They sat on the comfortable chairs—a couch and two big

easy chairs that had a low table at their center. They were on the edge of the sand pit so the entire family could unwind after the long day—dragons and humans alike—together.

Isabelle was getting more nervous as time went on. The sweet herbs in her tea calmed her a bit, but the underlying tension was definitely fraying her nerves.

Were the men not going to make a move? Were they waiting for her to initiate something? If so, she didn't think she could. She didn't have that kind of courage about her own femininity yet—if she ever would. Sex was so new. She had enjoyed it immensely, but she was still very much the novice. She had no idea how to initiate a sexual encounter. Especially not one that would involve all three of them.

"Try to relax, sweetheart," Robert said quietly. "I can see the tension in your shoulders from here. Nothing is going to happen tonight."

"What?" she blurted out, embarrassed a second later by the loud tone of her voice. She'd made the dragons stir. Four jewel-like eyes blinked open and stared at her.

"The four of us discussed this," Robert told her. "We are going to war tomorrow. We cannot give you the kind of experience you deserve—that we all deserve—for our first time together as a trio. For one thing, we don't have the time. It would be irresponsible of Bear and I to stay up all night for our own selfish purposes when our brethren will be expecting us to be sharp and ready to fight tomorrow."

Bear picked up the explanation. "Once we start something, we probably won't want to stop for a good long while. It's unrealistic to think we could easily turn our passions on and off like a tap. And you deserve better than some rushed joining. You are too special to us, Isabelle. We cannot treat you with such disregard. It goes against our natures, and our need to protect you in every way."

Their words impressed her. They overwhelmed her a bit too. And made her a little angry. There was a certain amount of taking things for granted included in their reasoning that annoyed her a bit, but then again, she had given them reason to believe she'd be up for anything they wanted. Hadn't she been sitting there fully expecting to participate in a trio session only moments before?

She was honest enough with herself to admit that they had a right to make assumptions about her participation. She was easy for them, as for no other man. Men. Although it still boggled her mind to think that she could have them both, when she didn't think too hard about it, it was beginning to feel somewhat natural. It's only when she had time to reflect on normal relationships—how *normal* was defined in her village—that she still had serious misgivings.

But everything was different in the Lair. Everything seemed possible here, in this magical place. Her nervous anxiety was being replaced by a sense of both disappointment and warmth that they would give so much thought to her feelings, as well as their own safety.

"We hope you understand," Growloranth spoke into their minds. *"It was Tildeth and I that first raised our concerns with our knights. As much as my mate and I wish to be together again, we would not see you cheated of the care you deserve."*

"Even we can see that you are new to all of this," Tilly put in. *"Some things should not be rushed. And we all have work to do on the morrow. This time—as it will be many times in the future—our duty to Draconia must come before our own desires. For what it's worth, I'm sorry, Isabelle, but I also believe in my heart that there will be time to complete our family after this battle is over. And I also believe that you will be more secure in your decisions if you have time to think them through. You might also benefit from talking more with Lady Silla. She is one of the most sensible women I know."*

When put that way, it made a lot of sense. Who was Isabelle to argue with the wisdom of two elder dragons? And their words also brought home the fact that they would be riding into danger tomorrow morning. Without her.

She had been so worried about the possible encounter that night that she had managed not to think about the danger coming in the morning, when the dragons and their knights would face a herd of angry, venom-spitting skiths. And once they were done with the skiths, there was an enemy army to deal with. Not good.

"I know this all must sound as if we are taking your agreement for granted." Robert addressed the bit that had annoyed her at first. "Truly, we are not. We will try our hardest never to take anything for granted if we are granted the blessing of having you as our mate. You must realize by now that we are very serious about the fact that you are the woman we want to complete our circle, to be our mate and join our family. We want that and our dragon partners want it as well."

Tilly's head bobbed up and down in agreement. *"I can see you nurturing my offspring as you would your own, and I have the greatest respect for your courage and tenacity, for having survived all by yourself for so long out on the edge of the woods. You are a brave and capable female that I would be proud to call sister. I hope, as we get to know each other better, you will feel the same about me."*

Now Isabelle was back to being overwhelmed. "You do me a great honor, Lady Tildeth. If the Mother of All wills it, I promise to do my best to be worthy of your faith in me."

Tilly nodded deeply as the significant moment passed between them. It brought home to Isabelle again all that she would gain if she joined with these knights. She would be able to live in this incredible place, with these wonderful people, and have dragons as friends. It was almost too much to believe.

But the crux of the matter was love. She would be loved—although they hadn't spoken the words yet—by two honorable men. And she would love them in return.

She was pretty sure about her feelings for both Robert and Bear, but did they love her? Neither of them had said so. Would they? Did men say such things, or was she supposed to figure it out on her own?

That would have to be the deciding factor. If they could love her, and she was more certain of her love for them, she would say yes. But she wasn't at that point yet. She needed time to figure a few things out.

It seemed the men and dragons had been way ahead of her in knowing what she needed.

"I thank you all for thinking of me. You're right. I do need time to think and process everything that's happened. I didn't quite realize it before, but I see the sense in what you've said. I'll also admit that the thought of you all going off to fight tomorrow morning is now at the forefront of my mind, and I don't like it one bit." A little bit of panic bled into her voice near the end of her statement and she saw Robert and Bear get up, coming over to sit on either side of her on the wide couch.

Robert put an arm around her shoulders while Bear took her hand in his.

"Take away one worry and another moves in to take its place," Tilly mused from the sand pit.

"Lady Isabelle," Growloranth said in a serious but gentle tone. *"This is one of the many things you must carefully consider. We are soldiers. Knights and dragons, all of us are sworn to fight on behalf of our country and peoples. If you agree to join our family unit, this will be part of your life. The reality is that we go off to fight and you'll have to stay here. You can be of help here, as you helped Lady Silla prepare her remedies for when we or our brethren get hurt."*

"You can bespeak dragons, so you can be of great help to those left behind when knights are unable to interpret for their partners due to injury." Growloranth added.

"It is chaotic in the Lair when we are called to fight," Tilly said. *"I know you can be of great help here. Every fighting force needs support. You could be part of our support system, if you so choose. It would help pass the time while waiting for us to come back, and you could talk to returning dragons and knights to learn first-hand what is going on at the battle site."*

Isabelle hadn't thought of that, though she had already decided to offer any assistance she could to Lady Silla and whoever else might be willing to let her do something. Doing something—anything—was far preferable to just sitting around, waiting for word.

"I am more than willing to help in any way that I can,"

Isabelle told them. "And I have every confidence in you all, but I cannot help but worry. Forgive me. It is not an indictment of you or your skills, merely my own insecurity. I would not like to lose any of you."

"You won't," Robert was quick to assure her, squeezing her shoulders. "We are two of the best fighters in the Lair and our partners are seasoned veterans. We have been through many battles together and we are still here to tell the tale. Tomorrow will be no different."

"I like your confidence, but I will still worry until I see you safe back here after the battle." She hugged Robert with one hand while Bear still held the other. She released Robert, then turned to hug Bear as well. "Please promise me you will be careful."

"I solemnly swear it, my heart," Bear promised as he held her close. "We will take no undue risks. Not when we know you will be here, awaiting our return."

She let him go and sat back, reaching for Robert's hand. Still holding Bear's with her other hand, she sat between them, surrounded by their warmth.

"Forgive me for worrying. I've only just found you and I don't want to lose either one of you before we have a chance to figure out what could be between us."

"Then you're saying there's a chance?" Robert asked quickly, a bright smile on his handsome face.

"Of course there's a chance. You already knew that. I am not the kind of woman to lie with both of you without being serious about this," she defended her own honor with a bit of humor in her tone.

"Yes, we knew," Bear agreed. "You are one in a million, Isabelle. We will give you all the time you need to be sure."

They slept together that night, in the huge bed in the mates' chamber, but they did not make love. All three were clothed in soft sleeping clothes and tucked under the blanket, though the men did spoon Isabelle between them. It was a comforting feeling, and so very warm. Isabelle had spent too many winter nights freezing in her cold cottage on the edge of the woods not to appreciate the warmth two men and two dragons could generate.

The men and dragons flew off just before dawn with all-too-brief kisses and words of reassurance. They promised her to be careful numerous times and their dragons were made to agree to it as well. Only then would Isabelle let them leave, though she went to the ledge with them, to see them off. It was before dawn and she shivered in the cold wind swept in by the repeated beats of the wings of launching dragons.

The entire Lair was going out to fight the skiths. It was a magnificent sight to see, though she quickly lost sight of the dragons in the pre-dawn darkness beyond the well-lit ledges. Still, she was surprised at just how many dragons and knights lived in this Lair. She stood in an out of the way spot, watching until the last dragon had left.

"Lady Isabelle." A woman's voice came from behind her and Isabelle turned to find the younger princess—Princess Belora—waving to her. Isabelle walked quickly over to her, not wanting to keep royalty waiting.

"What can I do for you, your highness?"

"First of all, call me Belora. I wasn't always a princess. I lived rough on the land up until just a few years ago when I met Gareth and Lars," she explained. "Silla said you might be willing to help when the casualties start coming in."

"I will do whatever you ask. In fact, I'd prefer a task rather than just sitting around worrying." Isabelle decided to be frank with the rather surprising princess.

Belora put one hand on Isabelle's forearm. "I know exactly what you mean. Don't worry, there is plenty to do. It's surprising, actually, how much the unmated knights do around here. When they're not around, the rest of us have a lot of slack to pick up." She smiled and tucked her arm into Isabelle's, starting them both walking toward the great hall, which was right down the corridor.

Isabelle spent the next few hours helping prepare food for the entire Lair. The regular menu was replaced by quick things that would be easily eaten on the go, in case the battle lasted longer than expected. Small, pastry-wrapped bits of meat and cheese went into the ovens by the tray full. Isabelle helped by cutting the ingredients to size while Belora crimped the edges of each filled pastry. They chatted as they worked, and Isabelle got to know Belora a bit better.

For royalty, she was really a very down to earth woman. Belora told her about how she met her mates and her adjustment to the idea of having two mates. She also talked about raising her young family—human babies and dragonets side by side.

They ate breakfast together and Silla joined them, claiming Isabelle for the rest of the morning, which they spent preparing the things that might be needed to treat injured dragons and knights. Bandages, toweling, clean linens and swabs all needed folding and sorting, along with the various salves and potions Silla had made ready.

They moved the bulk of Silla's herbal preparations from her workroom to a table set up in an open area on the main landing ledge. If a dragon was injured and made it back to the ledge, they wouldn't want to wait for him or her to go any farther before beginning treatment.

"Plus, the first thing to do when dealing with skith venom burns is to irrigate the area. See those cisterns over there?" Silla explained as they walked closer to the actual ledge. "And the channels carved into the floor that slope downward to the edge? The idea is that you can douse a dragon with water to dilute the skith acid and the water will run off the ledge through those channels. Every Lair has them, just in case. And the cisterns are kept full and refreshed each time it rains. There are collection areas up top that funnel down into the walls. Behind the vessels you see that are for everyday use, there are hollowed-out vats where vast quantities of rainwater are kept in readiness. Plenty to bathe the entire Lair full of dragons if need be."

Isabelle marveled again at the ingenious design of this amazing place. Other tables had been set up by some of the youngsters along the walls. Silla and Isabelle oversaw the placement of her supplies around the landing ledge, creating sets of items they might need, including sharp, clean blades, piles of clean cloths of various sizes, pots of the burnjelly they had prepared, needles and thread for stitches, and all sorts of medicinal herbs and prepared salves that might be useful.

Just before they were going to catch a quick bite of lunch, the first dragons limped back to the Lair. It was a young pair with newly-chosen knights who had only been training together for a few months. They had never fought skiths before and had made some rookie mistakes, according to the dragons who were both injured and embarrassed. Isabelle introduced herself and talked to the dragons while Silla and the two princesses worked at healing them.

Isabelle toted water and helped wash off the skith venom. Luckily, neither of the young dragons was hurt too badly. They wouldn't fly again today, but they would heal and be back to full strength soon. Once they were treated, Isabelle listened to the dragons and knights speak of the battle they had just left.

There were many skiths, which wasn't good, but the dragons were holding their own against the ground-bound creatures. The young dragons eventually limped under their own power to their quarters, but the knights stayed on the ledge knowing their help might be required by more seriously injured dragons and knights.

And sure enough, it wasn't long before two more dragons flew in, one of them just barely making the ledge before he collapsed. Isabelle immediately started sluicing the dragon's terrible injuries with water. She poured water on the burns to dilute the acid still eating away at the dragon's scales, skin and muscle.

Belora came over then, and Isabelle was shocked to realize that the young princess was a true healer. She had the gift, and something in her magic tingled against Isabelle's senses as she called forth her power and started working on the dragon's badly mangled foreleg. Isabelle watched, irrigating the dragon's burns and keeping out of Belora's way as much as possible, while fascinated at what the princess was doing.

When the lesser wounds were free of the acid taint, Isabelle went quietly to work on them, using the burnjelly and other medicines Silla and she had prepared. She knew from her mother's teachings that true healing took a lot out of the healer. It was better to keep such abilities for the really important injuries that might otherwise maim or kill a dragon, and stick to the more traditional remedies for the things that weren't life threatening. Isabelle kept a careful eye on Belora while they both worked on the auburn-colored dragon. When the princess was nearing the end of her work, Isabelle was at her side, ready to support her.

Sure enough, Belora teetered on her feet when she came out of the healing, but Isabelle was there to steady her. Belora gave her a surprised look and checked over the rest of the dragon's injuries.

"You've done good work here, Isabelle," Belora finally said when the dragon had been made as comfortable as possible. He would not be moved for some time, as his wounds were too severe and he was unconscious. "Thank you for catching me. You've seen true healing before, haven't you?"

Isabelle saw no reason to hide the truth from these people. While she would never breathe a word to the villagers, the people in the Lair were very different.

"My mother had a small gift, but her mother was a true healer, or so she told me." Isabelle missed her mother, but it felt somehow good to speak of her again, especially with people who she would have liked. "But she healed with song. Healing chants," Isabelle said, remembering the long winter evenings when her mother taught her of such things by the fire in their lonely cottage.

"Do you know the way of such things?" Belora asked, apparently interested.

"She taught me the words, but I've never used them. Well,

not out in the open," Isabelle admitted. "On rare occasions, when I work with the village's animals and I'm alone, I have been known to hum under my breath. It has a calming effect on the beasts." Isabelle smiled and knew Belora understood what she was saying.

Belora was about to say something when a dragon's cry of anguish sounded. A new pair was coming in for a landing and one of the knights was barely hanging on. As the dragon landed, his knight slid from his back, unconscious on the floor, a trail of blood smearing along his dragon's back.

Belora and Isabelle ran to help. Isabelle sluiced the dragon, who had areas of burned flesh along his side, while Belora looked at the knight. Silla and Adora came over and worked on him too, while Belora tried to calm the frantic dragon.

Isabelle couldn't figure why Belora wasn't using her magic on the knight. Clearly, he was in very bad shape and could use all the help he could get. Belora beckoned her over and Isabelle stepped carefully around the agitated dragon.

"Now would be a very good time for you to try out one of those healing chants at full volume, Lady Isabelle. My healing ability only works on dragons."

Isabelle was surprised, but filed that information away for later examination. The knight was dying and she had to at least try the things her mother had taught her. Isabelle began to chant, digging her toes into the stone beneath her feet and calling on the energy of the Mother of All to aid her in her quest to bring comfort to the gravely injured man.

For the first time in her life, Isabelle sang her chant at full volume within the vicinity of people—dragons and men— who were badly hurt. She had no idea what would happen. Perhaps nothing. But perhaps she would be able to help them in some small way. She clung to that thought. That small glimmer of hope.

She began to build the chant into something more substantial, just as her mother had taught her. It began to flow out of her and into the air around her. She could almost see the energy floating through the air from her mouth to the injured knight.

Isabelle was only peripherally aware that everyone on the ledge had stilled. Tranquility was part of her chant and if that sense of peace was imparted to those in pain or distress, she counted that as a good thing. Right now, her focus was on the man who lay dying between Silla and Adora's working hands. She reached for his fading spirit with her song and cradled him in the chant, not allowing him to leave, using the ancient words to bind him to his body and imparting some of the Goddess's energy into him, to sustain him while the healers did their work.

Buoyed by the power she could feel flowing through her at full strength for the first time in her life, Isabelle did all she could think of to help the knight. He was no longer dying and that brought a sense of satisfaction.

When she thought he was safely ensconced in his own body again, she drew back, taking the thread of energy the chant wrought with her, allowing it to spread around the ledge again before she finally ended her song. A stunned silence greeted her when she closed her mouth.

And then it was like everyone began talking at once, only they were using hushed voices and low murmurs. And they were looking at her with wide eyes.

"Milady," the dragon behind her spoke into her mind for the first time. This was the dragon who had brought the badly injured knight in. This was his partner. *"Thank you, milady. You saved him and I will be forever grateful. I did not believe Tildeth when she claimed you had the blood of the Fair Folk in your lineage, but I have seen the truth of it here today. Thank you for sharing your gift with my knight."* The dragon bowed its great head to her and Isabelle was overwhelmed by both his words and his gesture. Dragons bowed to no one. Well, very few people, at any rate.

"Sir..." she addressed him, not knowing his name, "...you do me too great an honor."

Belora touched her hand. "He's right though." The princess's words startled Isabelle into looking at her. "You have magic in your voice, Isabelle. It's unlike any I have heard or felt before. It is potent and pure, and of the Lady. Thank you for saving this knight's life, for without your chant, he would have left us."

"I—" Isabelle was about to protest again, but she remembered what she had felt and seen while she'd been using the chant. She stopped talking, unsure of what to say. She simply waved her hands in the air and then fled to man the water buckets as another dragon flew in, needing help.

Slowly, the rest of the gathering on the ledge went back to work. After a while, the moment passed and they were almost overwhelmed by dragons and knights with burns that needed treatment.

Then Growloranth flew in. He was hurt, and so was Robert. Her heart in her throat, Isabelle ran to them, dumping water over Growloranth's burns as she looked for Robert.

And then he was there, taking her shoulders, but keeping her at arm's length. She understood. His leathers were smoking with the pungent acid of skith venom.

CHAPTER NINE

"Come with me quickly, we'll wash you off." She tugged him toward one of the small areas set aside nearer the cisterns where they could rinse off people and things that came into contact with the acidic venom. In that spot, the contaminated water would be caught in the channels and sent down the side of the mountain, away from the Lair.

"It's only on the leather, except for one spot," Robert claimed, already unbuckling his armor as he walked. "Growloranth needs help more—" he began, but she cut him off.

"And he's getting it. Both princesses are seeing to his burns, which is more than enough. They are dragon healers."

"Yes, I know. Ouch!" he exclaimed as his armor came away and good piece of his shirt with it.

"Is that the only spot where the venom got through your armor?" she asked, already gauging the depth of the wound on his shoulder. It wasn't too bad and would heal well if they got water and then burnjelly on it immediately.

He chucked the contaminated armor to the side and bent over near the basin she indicated. The last thing they wanted to do was spread the venom all over his body. Better to rinse just the affected area at first, until they had diluted the acid sufficiently. He knew the drill, apparently, and cooperated as she poured bucket after bucket of water over his shoulder.

"Sweet Mother of All, that stings!" he exclaimed as the water sluiced over his raw skin.

"I'm sorry," she whispered.

"Don't worry. I know it has to be done," he gasped. "Keep going. It's starting to dissipate."

"Good. That means we've diluted it substantially. You should rinse your whole body off, in case there are spots we haven't noticed yet," she advised him. "The shoulder doesn't look too bad."

Robert stood and simply stripped off to his skivvies right there, without any hesitation at all. Isabelle felt her cheeks flame as he stood there, practically naked. He moved toward a station that had been set up for just this purpose and opened the tap near his head that would rain water down through a pipe that had a ceramic head on the end of it with multiple small holes. The effect was that of a rain shower. He moved under it and turned his body to be sure was completely washed off, including his head and hair.

When he was done, he closed the tap and reached for one of the many clean towels that had been stacked nearby. He dried himself off and came back to her.

"How's Growloranth?" he demanded even before allowing her to treat his wound. It had only been a matter of minutes since he'd come in and Growloranth was already being treated. Isabelle had been keeping tabs on both males.

"He's doing fine. No lasting damage. They are finishing up with him as we speak. Now, let me tend your shoulder, Robert. You need to be ready to fly when he is."

That got through to the handsome knight. He sat on the stool that she had set near her supply table and presented her with his injured shoulder. She noted that he positioned himself so that he could look out over the wide ledge to where Growloranth lay, being treated as well. When Robert didn't speak to her, she assumed he was communing silently with his dragon partner. She looked at his wound, deciding on the best course of treatment. Burnjelly would do, she thought, and began applying it over the area.

He sighed in relief as the burnjelly started to take effect.

"Thank you for taking care of him," came Growloranth's voice in her mind as she worked on Robert.

"No need for thanks. I could do no less. How are you feeling? Is there anything I can do to help?" she answered back.

"I am well enough now. The princesses have seen to the worst of my wounds and Lady Silla will handle the rest. Just take care of Robert. He would neglect himself if you were not here."

"Not on my watch." She winked at the dragon who lay several yards away, and he blinked one of his large, jeweled eyes at her in return. They had an understanding. *"What happened to get you two into such a state? And where were Tildeth and Bear when this happened? Do you think they're all right?"* She carefully sent her words to both Robert and Growloranth.

"They were running high guard reconnaissance, feeding Jared and Darian intelligence so they could run the battle plan," Robert explained in a tired voice.

"They saw us engage a knot of skiths. They knew we were on our way back here after we got burned," Growloranth added. *"But they were fine the last we saw them. Unlikely to be used on the ground because of their usefulness in the sky."*

Isabelle finished with Robert's treatment and was about to comment when she heard the trumpeting call that meant another dragon was coming in for a not-so-well-controlled landing. There had been quite a few skidding, hopping landings on the ledge today as injured dragons did their best to make it back home for treatment.

Isabelle and Robert both rushed to help in any way they could, but it proved unnecessary. The dragon landed and Isabelle saw it was Sir Gareth and his dragon partner, Kelvan, one of Princess Belora's mates. He didn't dismount, but reached a hand down for her. She climbed up on Kelvan's back as word spread silently from dragon to dragon.

Growloranth told them what was happening.

"The skiths have been defeated, but the enemy troops are now firing on our forces with diamond-tipped weapons. Two dragons have been shot

out of the sky and Princess Belora is going with Gareth to treat them enough so they can fly home."

"Diamond-tipped weapons?" Isabelle repeated, wondering why that was significant.

Robert took her hand and squeezed gently. "Diamond is the only edge sharp enough and strong enough to cut through dragon scale."

"Sweet Mother of All!" she whispered, shocked. She had believed dragons were the next best thing to invincible. The idea that they could be shot down made her gasp. Especially knowing that Tilly and Bear were out there, flying reconnaissance. "*Did he say who was shot down?*" she asked Growloranth quickly.

"*No, he did not, but I fear my mate is among the fallen,*" Growloranth replied solemnly. "*And I cannot fly to her aid. The Princess Adora forbade it. And truth to tell, I do not have the strength.*"

Both Isabelle and Robert ran to Growloranth's side. Tears were streaking out of his large, jewel-like eyes, rolling down his scaled skin to harden on the ground into a small pile of sparkling gems. How something so beautiful could come out of such heartbreak was beyond her comprehension, but that was unimportant now. What was important was the pain the dragon and his knight—and Isabelle too, if she was being honest—were feeling.

"I am with you, my old friend. Tildeth will be all right. You would know it if she wasn't." Robert stroked the dragon's neck, leaning against him, offering comfort in whatever way he could.

Isabelle reached out to touch the dragon's face. She had never dared to touch him before, but this was a dire circumstance. Her heart opened and the dragon stepped inside, his pain reaching out to her.

She stared into his eyes and simply stood with him, a hum of power passing between them. And then it became a real hum, in her throat, begging for release. Before she knew it, she was humming a tune of calm and peace. A sacred chant that would bring comfort until they knew for certain what was happening out on the battlefield.

Little by little all frantic activity on the ledge calmed. Anxiety was banished and Isabelle felt the world still. She eased her chant and drew back some of the power, knowing the injured dragons needed more than those who were treating them. She found she could control the direction and amount of calming energy she sent out into the area. She saved the best for Growloranth, calming his anxiety while they awaited news.

And then the bugling call of Tildeth reached their ears. She was landing.

It wasn't graceful and it was far from pretty, but she made it home.

Growloranth used what little strength he had left to crawl over to her side, staying out of the way of the healers, but managing to twin his neck with his mate's in greeting while he looked over her injuries for himself. She had a slash that went up one leg and over her belly. It had probably gone through her wing as well. The wing showed signs of recent healing, but the wound on her leg and body were still in need of attention.

Adora and Silla busied themselves at her side. Silla used her skills to clean and prepare the wound while Adora called on her magic to begin healing it. She couldn't heal it completely in one session, but she could give it a good start, and stop the worst of the bleeding.

Robert stayed by Growloranth's side while Isabelle went to help Silla, handing her whatever she needed, when she needed it. At one point, Silla grabbed her hand.

"A little calm wouldn't hurt right now," she said. Isabelle understood.

She began chanting quietly while they worked and the calm spread to Tilly. Isabelle added a verse to her chant to dull the dragon's pain while the healers did their work.

A little tingle shot through her when Isabelle's magic met Adora's, but they were compatible. The magics blended at the seam where they met, but didn't dissipate each other. In fact, they seemed to augment each other a little bit.

Adora caught her eye and smiled as she went back to work. It took quite a while, but between all their efforts, Tildeth's blood stopped flowing all over the landing ledge and her wound began to close. It took a moment before Isabelle realized Tilly was going to survive.

The relief she felt was so intense, she almost lost her footing as her chant ended. She realized in that moment that she cared a lot more than she'd thought for Tilly...and Growloranth. She loved them both as friends, or older, far wiser siblings.

And, she realized in an almost blinding flash of insight, she loved their knights. Period. She just loved them. Which reminded her...

"Where's Bear?" she whispered.

Tilly must have heard her question, for her deep, feminine voice came into Isabelle's mind a moment later. *I could not carry him with my injury and he was hurt as well. The spear got me, but he was hit by an arrow. They were seeing to his wounds and will bring him here as soon as it is safe.*

Isabelle's heart ached. She wanted to go to him, but there was no way. She would have to trust to his comrades—and Belora—to make sure he made it. Robert's arm came around her shoulder and pulled her back against him. He rested his chin atop her head and surrounded her in his warmth.

She clung to him, sharing the worry over their missing man. She tried sending a message directly to Bear's mind, but he was too far away.

"I cannot bespeak him," she whispered, clinging to Robert's arm.

"Neither can I, but don't worry. He is simply out of range," Robert assured her.

Tilly raised her head and looked at them. *He may be, but there are dragons flying between here and the battle. I will ask one to act as relay.* She closed her eyes and almost immediately opened them again. *He is near!* She sounded excited. *He is unconscious but being carried on the back of old Algath. Look for a green dragon. He should be here any minute. "*

Tilly's head swung around, looking eagerly toward the landing ledge though she couldn't move while the healers were still working on her injuries. Isabelle went as close as she dared to the busy ledge, not wanting to be in the way, but straining her eyes to see if she could pick out a green dragon in the blue sky.

"There!" Robert breathed excitedly. He was right behind her. "I see him."

"Bear?" Isabelle whispered.

"No, I see Algath. But there is more than one knight on his back. Good ol' Algath. See over there?" Robert pointed past her ear and she followed the line of his arm to the correct portion of the sky. Sure enough, there was a green dot moving rapidly closer and resolving from dot into very large dragon. Algath had an extra large wingspan.

Within moments, the large green dragon landed nearby. A knight jumped down off his back and reached up for Bear, who was slung across the dragon's back, unconscious. Robert moved to assist, despite his shoulder injury, as did a number of other people. Princess Adora was still working her healing magic on Tildeth, but Silla rushed to Bear's side, as did Isabelle.

She saw at once that Bear had a hastily wrapped wound on his lower left leg, but the more worrying gash was on his right temple. It was the head wound that had caused his unconscious state, in all probability. The leg wound was still bleeding, but it wasn't too bad. It could be stitched up and healed in a few weeks time. Less, if a bit of magic was used.

Silla went to work while Isabelle assisted, handing the healer things as she asked for them.

"A bit of your chanting wouldn't go amiss, if you have the energy," Silla took a moment to say as Isabelle handed her a clean towel.

Isabelle thought about which of the variations her mother had taught her to use and decided on the best for this case. She centered herself and a moment later, began to hum the melody, building into the actual song of the chant by slow degrees, stirring the power that dwelled in all living things to aid her in her work.

It took a while, but by the time Silla was finished sewing up Bear's leg, he was starting to wake up. Isabelle stood near his head and had sung her chant throughout, using clean water and cloths to bathe the shallow wound on his temple. She had rubbed some healing salve on lightly and then covered the cut with a bandage. She had then wrapped another thin strip of cloth around Bear's head, to hold the wad of clean linen in place.

"Isabelle?" Bear's whisper caught her attention.

"I'm here," she said, ending the chant and allowing the magic it had called and directed, to dissipate. "Quiet now. You are in the Lair. Safe and sound."

"Tilly?" he asked. "My head is killing me. Can't seek her with my mind."

"She's right over there, watching everything. Princess Adora just finished working on her and said that she'll be good as new given a few days rest. Growloranth too. He came in with Robert a short while before Tilly arrived. Everyone's going to be fine."

"Robert?"

"I'm here, my friend," Robert said, moving closer. He had been hovering in the background, ready to help.

The men spoke a bit while relief rushed through Isabelle's veins. She had been so worried. More worried than she should have been if these men and dragons meant nothing to her, or were merely friends. No, she had realized something vital during those hours of waiting, and then the agony of seeing them hurt.

The simple truth was, she loved them.

All of them. The dragons as well as their knights. Certainly the love in her heart for the dragons was different than the love she felt for the men, but it was no less real. And if the men asked her again, she would say yes to being their mate, even though the idea of a triple mating still scared her.

Isabelle felt a touch on her elbow as she stood back, watching Robert and Bear talk. She turned to find Princess Adora behind her.

"Your magic is potent and healing," the older lady of royal blood began. "Thank you for sharing your gift with us today. If your Robert and Bernard haven't already asked you to stay, please consider this a formal invitation to make your home among us, whether or not you wish to mate with any of our knights. A gift like yours is meant to be used, and we will always make room in our Lairs for people with good hearts who can bespeak dragons and are willing to help."

Isabelle was flattered. And honored beyond words.

"I would like to stay," she whispered, with only minor hesitation.

Adora touched her shoulder, squeezing gently as she smiled. "Good. I'll keep it quiet until the boys come up to scratch. Sometimes, I have learned, it is best to let the men think certain things were their idea." She gave Isabelle a conspiratorial wink. "But I wanted you to know that you are wanted here regardless of what happens between you, Robert and Bernard. You have options now, Isabelle. You are not alone."

The impassioned words moved Isabelle to tears, and Adora gave her a quick hug of support. There weren't a lot of tears, but a few slipped free to run down Isabelle's cheeks. Robert apparently saw because a moment later he was back at her side, his arm around her shoulders.

"It's okay, sweetheart," he crooned. "We're all going to be okay. And we have you to thank for it." He bent down to kiss her cheek, rubbing his lips against her temple and snuggling close for a moment. "You have been so good to us today. Never have we had anyone special waiting for us when we returned from battle. While I don't like that you were worried, it made it easier for us knowing we had you to come home to."

At that point, the tears hit her again. The loneliness she thought she heard in his voice touched her heart. Here were men—a Lair full of them—willing to put their lives on the line for a country and people who had no real idea of how they lived. She had noticed how most of the knights in this Lair were single. Some had fighting partners, if their dragons were established mates, but most had no wife, which meant their dragons could not consummate their union and the knights were searching, looking for the woman who might complete their family and bring them all together.

She understood so much she had never even contemplated before. Dragons and knights were just a fact of life if one lived in Draconia, even though most people never had contact with either. Certainly, the common folk didn't have a clue how the knights and dragons lived, except to know that there were things called Lairs positioned strategically around the country.

This Lair—the Border Lair straddling the border between Draconia and the neighboring country of Skithdron—had hundreds of knights and dragons living in it. The place was mostly male, though there were a number of women who were mated to sets of knights, and even a few children, both human and dragon. The children she had seen were parented by both sets of adults in the family—human and dragon—too. It was a fascinating partnership that Isabelle found kind of beautiful.

The more she saw of the Lair and the lifestyle of those living here, the more she wanted to be part of it. There was just one thing holding her back now. She wasn't sure of Robert and Bear's feelings. She knew they cared, but she needed to hear the words. She needed to know for certain that they could truly love her.

She didn't want to be just their only choice because they had no one better to ask. She wanted to be their choice. Period.

And for that, she needed to hear those three little words— I love you—from both of them. Six words total. Was that too much to ask?

CHAPTER TEN

A week passed while the dragons and knights healed, then went back to duty. The village had to be cleaned up and the traitors dealt with. A constant presence of knights and dragons was required in Halley's Well and at the Valla Pass, to maintain security in the village and along the border.

The enemy forces had been beaten back and dealt a serious blow, but little skirmishes were still possible. Patrols had been stepped up and mountain passes up and down the border were being watched more carefully. Bear and Tilly were in high demand for their ability to fly during daytime hours without being seen. The only days they got any sort of respite was when rain threatened and dark clouds ruined Tilly's natural light camouflage.

While Bear and Tilly worked in the sky, Robert and Growloranth worked in the forest and village. Isabelle had asked about going back to see her home, but both men had objected, claiming it was still much too dangerous. Between duty and sleep, there wasn't a lot of time to spare. The two knights were either sleeping or working, and little else.

They had not tried to pressure Isabelle in any way—either for sex or for a decision on whether she would stay in the Lair with them. Things were at a standstill, with nothing decided. It was a difficult way to exist, but Isabelle had come to trust Lady Silla and had discussed her situation with the other woman a few times. Silla's advice had given her hope. And patience.

Isabelle knew she couldn't put her own needs in front of those of the Lair. Her men had a duty they must perform and she could not interfere with that. Coming to terms with that idea helped her get through the trying times. But finally, after ten days of no action on any personal issue, Isabelle had had enough.

The next rainy day, she promised herself, she was going to bring this situation to a head. So to speak.

She got her wish a day later, when storm clouds filled the skies and Bear and Tilly were given some time off from their reconnaissance flights. They were talking about going to the village and working alongside the knights and dragons who were still on patrol and clean-up duty. Robert and Growloranth were scheduled to do the same later in the day, but would be in the Lair for the morning at least.

Isabelle realized this was her chance. She got up her nerve and decided to enlist a little dragonish help.

"Lady Tildeth?" Isabelle sent silently to the female dragon. When the sky blue dragon's head rose from the sand pit at the center of their suite and Isabelle knew she had the female dragon's attention, she continued. *"I need your assistance. Can you convince Bear to stay here today? There is something we need to clear up, and there has been no time to do it. I know your duty comes first, but could you at least delay him so we can hash this out?"*

"Answer me one question first. Do you truly love my knight?" Tilly's pale aquamarine eyes pinned Isabelle where she stood.

Isabelle took a deep breath before answering honestly. *"I do. It's his feelings for me that we need to clarify."*

"Has he not told you?" Tilly looked confused in a way that only a dragon could.

Isabelle shook her head, a bit of her sadness and distress entering her mental tone. *"No, he hasn't."*

"Silly boy," Tilly commented in an indulgent, chastising

way. *"Never fear, we will get this straightened out. I think I feel a strain in my wing that needs to be seen to right away."*

Buoyed by Tilly's agreement to stay in the Lair this morning, Isabelle smiled and thanked the massive dragon who was now her partner in crime.

Bear went back to their suite a half-hour later, after seeing Tilly to Princess Adora's workshop. He was still shaking his head over what had happened there, but doing as he was told.

Robert was just eating a bit of toast, his day starting a lot later than Bear's, owing to the work schedules they had been assigned. Isabelle was sitting with Robert in the conversation area near the side of the dragons' wallow. Robert's plate was on the low table as he sat on one of the overstuffed chairs, and Isabelle was seated on the couch, facing him. Bear flopped down on another chair at the side of the arrangement, between them.

"I thought you would be long gone by now," Robert said around a mouthful of toast. "What's amiss?"

"Tilly said her wing was strained and wanted to have Princess Adora check it, but when we got to Adora's chamber, Growloranth showed up and all three of them told me to leave." Bear literally scratched his head in confusion.

"I was wondering where he'd gone," Robert said, finishing his toast.

"If I was a suspicious type of person, I might think they were plotting something," Bear finally voiced his concerns. Something about Tilly's supposed injury didn't seem right. Tilly was usually the last one to complain about anything.

"Your instincts are correct," Isabelle floored him by saying. Both Robert and he looked at her with surprise. "I asked Tilly to keep you here today, Bear."

He liked it when she called him Bear. She had stuck to using Sir Bernard for a very long time, but he didn't want any formality between them. In fact, he wanted nothing between them—as it had been that one glorious time when they had been together. But he and Robert had agreed. They wouldn't pressure her. And they wouldn't try to make love to her again unless they were all together.

Like now?

Bear started to consider the possibilities. Why did she want him to stay in the Lair today? Well. There was only one way to find out. He needed to ask her.

"Why?"

Robert beat him to the punch, but it was all right. They both needed to know what was on their potential mate's mind.

"Because I can't keep going like this," Isabelle said in a rush. Bear's heart almost stopped. Did she want to leave? "I need to know where we all stand and if we can make this work. I feel like you've been avoiding me the past few days. I know your duty comes first," her voice filled with tears and Bear wanted to go to her, but she held up a hand, palm outward, as if trying to hold them back until she was done with whatever it was she wanted to say. "I understand. But the past few days, things have quieted down. Everyone says so. And you have still been avoiding me. I need to know if you still want me or if you want me to go and are being too polite to say it to my face."

Bear was out of his chair and at her side within seconds. So was Robert, on her other side. Luckily, the couch was built for three.

"We want you here, Isabelle," Robert whispered, holding one of her hands. Bear took her other hand, squeezing gently.

"We really do," he added. "We don't ever want you to leave. We want you to be our mate."

Bear wasn't an eloquent man, but he knew when he needed to say certain things. This seemed to be their time of reckoning—engineered by the woman they wanted to be part of their lives forever. He wouldn't have thought she would ever be so bold, but he really liked it. He was so proud of her. She was finding her inner strength. That was something she would need if she was going to be their mate in truth.

"Why?" She echoed Robert's earlier question and Bear

was a bit confused.

Didn't she already know that they were destined to be together? Didn't she feel the same pull whenever they were near to each other? Didn't she know they loved her more than life itself?

A frisson of doubt crept over him. If she didn't feel those things, did it mean she wasn't their mate? Could they have fooled themselves so completely into believing she would feel the same things they did? Did she not care for them at all? Did she not love them—at least a little?

Bear's heart sank. He knew he had to lay it all on the line, but suddenly he was truly unsure of the entire situation. He could lay his feelings bare and be rejected.

But he had to do it. He had to try. He took a deep breath and plunged in, knowing this time, Robert would be even more reticent than he was to take that final step.

Bear reached out and stroked her hair, drawing her attention to him, holding her gaze with his own. She was so beautiful to him.

"Why do we want you to be our mate?" he repeated the crux of her question, gently. "I can speak only for my own feelings, though I'm pretty sure Robert feels the same. I want you to stay because...I love you. I will love you for the rest of my days, whether you decide to share your life with us or not. You are the only woman in the world for me, and if you leave, my heart will shatter, never to be healed."

Tears welled in her eyes and he used his thumb to wipe away one that fell down her cheek. He tried to smile at her, even as his future hung in the balance.

Robert's hands settled on her shoulders and Bear let go of her face, knowing they could never be complete until both knights had committed to their mate. She turned to Robert and Bear silently encouraged his friend to seal the deal. Robert was the eloquent one. If he couldn't convince her to stay, then no one could.

Robert opened his mouth and then seemed to freeze.

"Tell her, you fool!" Bear sent urgently to his fighting

partner's mind.

Robert started as if he'd been poked. "I love you too," he blurted out.

Bear wanted to shake his head and groan. His supposedly silver-tongued partner didn't seem to have much to say. *Idiot.*

"I'll love you forever, sweetheart," Robert added, whispering as emotion filled his gaze.

And then Bear understood. Robert was so overcome with the intensity of his feelings, it scrambled his brain. That was the only excuse Bear could give him in this situation. Bear, on the other hand, was pushed by emotion to say things he normally kept inside. Love gave him courage, whereas it seemed to steal all of Robert's usual polish.

"You see what you've done to him?" Bear whispered, leaning close to Isabelle's ear. "I've never seen Robert at a loss for words. You did that to him. Loving you has wiped away all the pretense, and left him speechless. And it seems to have given me the freedom, for once, to say what's in my heart." Bear turned her head with one finger under her chin and kissed her deeply.

When they broke apart, he saw the happy tears in her eyes and his heart rejoiced. "I love you with all my heart."

"I love you too. Both of you," she said, lifting his spirits and giving him confirmation that his love life was not about to end in a bright ball of flames.

"Then I think we have an accord," Bear dared to say. "Do you agree to be our mate?" He had to have the words, just as she had needed to hear them speak of their love plainly. So there could be no chance of confusion.

Isabelle's smile lit his world. "I do."

Happiness filled him as the realization hit. They were going to be a family. She loved them.

"Then I suppose we'd better start planning a mating ceremony," Bear said, thinking more about the wedding consummation than the actual ceremony.

"But we don't have to wait until then, right?" Isabelle said with a shy little smile that made him want to purr.

"No, milady," he agreed, moving closer to her on the couch and untying the closure at her neck that kept her blouse together. "As long as we all want the same thing, nothing is forbidden to us. You do want us, don't you?" Bear asked playfully as he noted the way her breathing hitched as he cupped her generous breasts in his hands.

"I do," she repeated her earlier agreement. "Sweet heaven, I do."

Her voice trailed off as he lowered his head and licked his way down over her throat to her breasts, playing there for a good long time. When he looked up sometime later, Robert had turned her head and claimed her mouth. The sight of his fighting partner kissing their mate was incredibly exciting.

Bear had known for a long time that he would end up sharing a mate with Robert—if they managed to find one—but they had never before shared a woman between them. That was something they had agreed to preserve for their mate alone. Bear was glad now that they had waited. Most knights didn't, but they had both wanted to keep something special for when they found their mate.

It was special all right. Bear had never felt the level of excitement that was riding him now. And the dragons weren't even involved yet. Bear could only guess at the frenzy their mating flight would induce in their human counterparts. All in all, it was a good thing that the three of them get a little practice in before the dragons reunited. Bonding with their mate now might mean the difference between having her join wholeheartedly in the mating flight frenzy—or being scared out of her wits by their possible aggression.

Neither Bear nor Robert knew how they were going to react when the backwash of lust from their dragon partners hit them. He hoped they would be able to keep their heads, but stories abounded in the Lair of near-mindless coupling inspired by dragons among the mated trios. With Isabelle so new to passion, Bear feared frightening her with the intensity that was said to develop to an inhuman height when the dragons became involved.

Better to start off slow. Well, as slow as they could manage. It felt like the three of them were about to reach heights of passion Bear had never quite realized existed. Just the fact that they were all together. Mates. He couldn't get over it, and that one thought added a new dimension to their time together that could never be replicated by any of the encounters he'd had up to this point.

Robert moved to the far corner of the couch, pulling Isabelle downward to lie with her back to his front, serving her up for Bear on a platter, as it were.

"You take the front this time," Robert sent to him privately. Bear could feel the tension in the words—the shaky control in his tone.

Bear rid Isabelle of the rest of her clothing, kissing his way down her body. Robert helped by serving up her breasts in his hands, holding them while Bear sucked at first one peak, then the other. When Bear moved lower, Robert continued to pluck at her distended nipples, making her writhe and moan in a most satisfying way.

Moving lower, Bear spread her legs and zeroed in on his target, smiling against her clit when she gasped as he licked her, then moved even closer. Nibbling on her most sensitive places, he was careful with her, but still strove to push her just a little bit higher with each movement.

When he stuck his tongue into her channel, her hips rose as she cried out, coming against his mouth. *Oh, yeah.* That's just what he wanted. He wanted to drive her out of her mind—into new realms of desire and lust—before they all joined in their first adventure as a trio.

He rode her through the small orgasm, gentling her with his hands on her hips. Then it was Bear's turn to move back to his corner of the couch, taking Isabelle with him.

She smiled at him when he pulled her over his body.

"Do I get to have my way with you now?" she asked playfully. Her eyes sparkled in a way that made him want to see that same expression on her face over and over again. He'd make it a goal.

"You can have your way with me any time you want, my heart," he replied, nearly groaning when her soft hands started to undress him.

He felt movement at the other end of the couch that told him Robert was getting ready for the next part of this encounter. They hadn't exactly planned this, so they were improvising. Still, one item in particular would make this all go a lot easier, and Robert was smart enough to go fetch it before they moved any farther along this path.

Meanwhile, Bear had to try to keep it together long enough for the triple joining they were working toward. With Isabelle's hands roaming all over his body as she undressed him, he wasn't entirely sure he'd be able to hold back.

"Better get a move on, Robert," Bear sent to Robert, who was making noise in his bedroom. It sounded like he was tossing things around, probably looking for what they needed.

"I can't find the jar," Robert sent back, his tone tinged with annoyance and a hint of panic.

"Get the oil in the bathing chamber. That'll work. Even cooking oil in the kitchen would work, for heavens sake."

"Right."

Bear could hear Robert's footsteps padding around the perimeter of the suite and then he was back, the couch dipping at the other end as Robert rejoined them. Isabelle was on her hands and knees, licking her way over Bear's bare chest in a shy, but determined way. He loved the feel of her hands on him and her mouth was driving him wild.

She squeaked and lifted her head when Robert touched her from behind. Bear couldn't see exactly what Robert was doing back there, but he had a good idea of what Robert was about. He was kneeling on the couch behind Isabelle, his hands at her hips, most likely spreading her cheeks and rubbing oil into her, to ease his way.

Isabelle nearly jumped out of her skin when she felt Robert's fingers slide between her cheeks from behind. They were slick with something. Some kind of oil, she guessed, and she knew what that meant now.

A little shiver of anticipation went through her at the memory of what she had experienced with Robert, when he'd taken her there. It had been unlike anything she could have expected, but she enjoyed it immensely. She had spent some time talking to Silla about intimate things and was prepared as best as she could be, for what her two knights might ask of her. Deep down, it was all a matter of trust. And she trusted Bear and Robert not to hurt her, or push her beyond what she could give them.

They loved her. That's what mattered most.

She pushed back into Robert's hand as he sought and gained entrance. It felt good. Almost better than she remembered. He didn't rush her, but he did increase the tempo and pressure, adding more fingers until she was rocking against his hand, seeking another release.

All it took was Bear's hands on her breasts to set her off again. She moaned and closed her eyes, enjoying the sensations that spiraled through her body.

The climax went through her and the men let her have it. Only when it began to dissipate did Robert change tactics. He removed his hand and a moment later, replaced his fingers with something more solid—more enticing. She felt his hard cock slide up into her, bit by bit, taking it slow, but demanding entrance she did not want to deny.

When he was fully seated inside her, he paused. She took a moment to bask in the sensation. Oh, that felt good. Full. Stretched. Exciting.

And then Bear pushed lightly, but firmly against her shoulders, raising her up so that Robert's chest was against her back, his rod firmly ensconced within her while he held her hips. Bear took a moment to gather some of the throw pillows, placing them in front of her—even going so far as to lift her knees and put a few under her, so she was a little higher. Perfect height, it turned out, for their possession.

Interesting. And inventive. She liked what they were doing and looked forward to see what might come next. She hoped it involved Bear's cock, but she was willing to wait and see which of the many variations Silla had told her about, they might choose.

After he seemed content with her placement, Bear rose to his knees in front of her. His hands went to her waist, caressing as he looked deep into her eyes.

"Are you all right?" he asked, melting her heart with his obvious concern.

"It's good," she replied, barely able to catch her breath. She wanted to scream for him to go faster. To get on with it. But she couldn't. This was a voyage of discovery and she had to be patient.

"I'm going to take you now, joining the three of us as one," Bear warned in a soft tone. "I want you to tell me right away if it's too much."

"I want it," she gasped as he moved closer, lifting her thigh to wrap around his hips. "I want you. Both of you."

And then he was there, at her entrance, stretched impossibly tight. But the pillows under her knees allowed her to move around a bit, making room for him. He pressed upward, joining their bodies and she felt the double possession Silla had told her about for the first time. It was...odd. Odd and incredibly exciting. Naughty in the best possible way.

"All right, baby?" Robert whispered in her ear from behind, the warmth of his moist breath in the shell of her ear making her shiver. Sensory overload was too mild a description of what she was feeling.

"Fine," she gasped, unable to speak more than a single syllable. She felt way more than just *fine*, though. She felt possessed. Taken. Liberated. Loved.

Both men made some adjustments to their position, moving her limbs and placing their hands at points to support her body. They took care for her comfort in a way that made her heart ache with love for them both.

And then they began to move. Bright stars in heaven! She hadn't known her body could produce such sensations. The quivers of desire started in her belly and shimmied up and down her spine.

She couldn't move much, but it didn't matter. Her men took care of her in the most delightful sort of way. They moved slow at first, watching her every move before increasing the pace little by little.

They took their time and made sure she was with them. She had never experienced such feelings of love, possession and abject desire before. She was new to lovemaking, but even she could sense this was something incredibly special. Just for them. Together.

She began to tremble and two pairs of arms were immediately there, supporting her. She wanted to cry at the beauty of the moment when she shattered, her shout of release echoing around the domed chamber.

But the men didn't come. They kept at her, moving incrementally faster, building her desire once again, driving her higher than she thought she could go. The climaxes built on each other as her whole body shook.

She was moaning when the pace picked up to a true frenzy. Her body was going far beyond what she'd ever dreamed was possible. The climax hit and just…stayed. Multiple orgasms wracked her body with almost indescribable pleasure. Only dimly did she hear the groans of her men, but she felt the warmth of their come when they finally reached their own peaks of pleasure within her.

Sweet Mother of All, that felt good.

Even as their frantic motion stilled, they cared for her. They disengaged carefully, after long moments, taking care not to strain her body in any way. They were both so strong, so caring. And they were hers. All hers.

EPILOGUE

Over the next two weeks, things settled down on the border. It looked like the enemy had been truly routed, and had tucked tail and run away. For now, at least.

The village of Halley's Well had been cleared of traitors and Isabelle had even been able to get Bear and Robert to promise to take her back there in a week or two to see what was left of her former home. They warned her she might not like what she found there.

She knew the skiths had done a great deal of damage, but she wanted to see it for herself, to bring herself some closure. Isabelle planned to make her home at the Lair from now on, but she wanted to see if there was anything of her former life she might still be able to salvage and bring back as a keepsake. A reminder of all that had come before to lead her to this current state of incredible happiness.

She visited her chickens often and she set up the kitchen in their suite to her liking. They had eggs for breakfast a few times each week thanks to the thoughtful gift Bear had given her all those days ago. Her little flock was doing just fine in their new environment.

The three of them made love each night, perfecting their moves and trying new ones. And Silla was helping Isabelle learn the dances she would need to perform at the mating ceremony that was being planned for the end of the week.

The dragons would take to the sky then, in their first mating flight since choosing Bear and Robert as their knights. Every joining they experienced was working toward that one—the big one where the dragons' passion would influence the knights into something unlike anything that had come before, if rumors and accounts from married knights were to be believed.

When the day of the mating celebration finally came, Isabelle was more than ready. She was primed and able to perform the required dances—each one more risqué as the night wore on. When the dragons took to the sky, mated trios all around the Lair joined their dragon partners in passion, the dragons' influence over their bonded partners so great, that the knights had to partake of their mate's passion, or go mad.

Isabelle was ready. More than ready, if truth be told. She received her men with enthusiasm and a certain sense of wellbeing that finally—finally—everyone in the extended family was made whole. The dragons' joy and love flared through the connection with Bear and Robert, and even Isabelle felt the wash of emotion and passion, sensitive as she was to magic and the two dragons involved, in particular.

She welcomed her mates into her body and the dragons' influence into her soul, and for a moment during the most incredible pleasure yet, she felt as if she too, was flying.

A day or two later, when the newlyweds finally felt like venturing out of their suite, they went to the great hall for a late dinner and found a somewhat raucous gathering of knights, their ladies, and even some of the children and workers who lived in the Lair. May of the dragons loitered nearby as well, and a many others filled sections of the great hall that had been cleared of tables and chairs.

Everyone was watching the small gathering by the hearth on one side of the giant chamber where various stews and beverages were kept ready at all hours for those on late duty.

A stunning pale orange-peach dragon lay to one side, a bronze-brown dragon next to her, their sinuous necks entwined. They were clearly a couple.

But it was the golden-haired knight standing in front of the dragons holding a lute that really captured Isabelle's attention.

"Ah, I see the newlyweds have come up for air," the golden-haired man stated with a smile that lit the room.

He had a charisma that was familiar to Isabelle as a path opened up between the trio at the door and the gathering by the hearth. Robert and Bear seemed to take the loud cheer that went up from the other knights in stride as they escorted her up to a place made for them right near the bard. To her surprise, the man put down his lute and came over to give both Robert and Bear back-pounding greetings filled with congratulations and good cheer.

"I'm sorry we had to miss the wedding, but I am thrilled to see you two looking so happy. I saw Tildeth and Growly on the way in and they told me all about your new addition to the family." Finally the vocal knight turned to greet Isabelle, taking her hand and bowing over it, placing a light kiss on her knuckles. His eyes met hers and she knew instantly she had met him before.

"I remember you," she whispered. "You were Jinn."

The man smiled as he raised his head and winked. "Indeed I am. We were both very young when our paths last crossed, but you are the image of your mother, and I remember her well. She taught me the lute fingering style of her people, which I still use to this day," he said, surprising Isabelle greatly. "I was very sad to learn of her passing." He squeezed the hand he still held, his expression darkening to convey his true regret and heartfelt feelings. Isabelle fought the tears she felt building behind her eyes. "You have my deepest condolences, milady."

"Thank you," she managed to whisper. "Are you the one they call Drake?"

His expression brightened slightly. "Indeed. I was known

as Drake of the Five Lands when I traveled as a bard, but I recently returned to my homeland, and Jenet over there made the horrid mistake of claiming me as her knight. Can you imagine?"

He finally let go of Isabelle's hand to gesture toward the gorgeous peach dragon behind him. Her head had risen over his shoulder, untwining with her mate so they could both look over the new arrivals.

The dragoness's voice entered Isabelle's mind. *"Would you mind telling me what you know of Drake's time abroad, sometime? I missed a lot of his life and I enjoy hearing about how he lived while he was away."*

Isabelle was surprised by the eager request, but glad to comply. *"It would be an honor, Lady Jenet, though I'm not sure how much help I'll be. I was very young and my memories of that time may not be the clearest."*

"Whatever you remember will be more than I know now," Jenet assured her. *"Drake was right. Your magic feels of the fair folk, though you are not full-blooded,"* Jenet observed. *"It is an honor to make your acquaintance."*

Now that was interesting. Dragons were quite formal, but the honor of being acquainted, so to speak, usually went the other way. Something strange was happening here, but Isabelle had no idea what it was.

"Likewise, milady," Isabelle replied politely.

She looked back to Drake and realized he had been watching her closely. He had an odd expression on his face as he drew a tall lady and another knight forward. He introduced his mate, Lady Krysta, and the third member of their trio, Sir Mace, as well as the other dragon in the family unit, Sir Nellin. Isabelle greeted them all as they were introduced, wondering why the entertainment had ground to a halt simply to make introductions.

She looked around briefly and realized that nobody seemed to mind. Everyone gathered in the great hall was broken into small groups that were sharing food and wine. A general feeling of relaxed celebration filled the place.

Drake invited Isabelle and her mates to sit at his table, which was on the far side of the hearth. The rest of the small gathering of musicians began to play a quiet tune while Drake took a break and joined his family, escorting Isabelle, Robert and Bear over to sit. The noise level in the hall was a low hum, with the music adding a festive air, but not overpowering the conversation.

Wine was passed around and toasts made to the newlyweds before Drake pinned Isabelle with his blue gaze once more. She thought she saw flames in the depths of his eyes, but that had to be a flight of fancy. He was very intent though, and she couldn't really understand why.

"How much do you remember of your origins, Lady Isabelle?" Drake asked suddenly, surprising her.

Isabelle stilled and put her wine goblet back on the table before answering. "Not much. Mama never spoke about the past."

"She spoke of it at least once," Drake said with quiet surety. "To the leader of the Black Dragon Clan of the Jinn. And the tale was passed to me because I hold a certain authority, even today, within my adopted Clan." Isabelle could see that even Sir Mace and Lady Krysta were intrigued by Sir Drake's words. As was Isabelle herself. What could he know that she didn't?

"What did she say?" Isabelle asked, her hands shaking. Robert put a comforting arm around her shoulders, while Bear's arm went around her waist. They were so good to her. They were her family now.

"Lady Isabelle, I'm not sure what you'll think of the tale I have to tell, but I can assure you that every word of it is true. The Jinn have the best network of spies in the world, and the story was checked out after your mother told it. The Jinn know it to be true, which is good enough for me."

"Sir Drake, you're scaring me. What is it that you know?" Isabelle asked.

"Do not be alarmed, milady. The news is not bad. Your mother was more than a traveling bard when she joined the

Jinn. She was a woman of noble—royal—blood, banished for having fallen in love with a human. Your mother was fey. She gave up her family and home to make a life with a human man, your father. But the fair folk are the next best thing to immortal, though as you know, they can die in certain ways. Your mother had only a few short decades with her true love before he began to grow old. You were born just before his reign was challenged. He fought the challenger and died. That's when Salomar rose to power in the North. And that's why your mother fled with you and took on a new identity, finally hiding you in obscurity here in Draconia. You are the rightful heir to the Northern throne—only daughter of King Eovar the Just."

"You've got to be joking," Isabelle protested, though she did remember her mother speaking of her father, occasionally slipping and calling him by name. On the rare occasional when she did that, she called him Eov. But there was no way...

"It is no joke, milady—or should I say, my princess," Drake assured her. "And your mother was of royal blood as well. She was the youngest daughter of a fey leader. Her name was Princess Sania and her father is King Teodorus of the Northern Reach. His lands lie to the north and west, neighboring the lands your father once ruled. As far as I know, he is still alive and still in power."

"*I knew it!*" Tilly's voice sounded through her mind. "*I knew you were fey, Isabelle. Didn't I say so when we first met?*"

"*Give her a moment to breathe, my love,*" Growloranth advised his mate openly. "*I'm sure this is a lot to take in all at once.*"

Isabelle was trembling and she didn't know what to think. Or what to say. She looked around, unsurprised to find Tildeth and Growloranth had been given room behind them. The whole Lair, it seemed, humored the newlyweds.

She caught Growloranth's eye and nodded her thanks. He nodded back, understanding.

"I'm..." she began, but faltered. She felt Bear's hand squeeze her waist in encouragement and support. How she loved him. And Robert. And her new dragon family. She didn't know what she would do—or where she would be—without them. They gave her strength just by their presence. "I'm overwhelmed," she finally got out.

Drake nodded gently. "I understand." He sat back, watching her. "I just thought it was about time you knew where you came from. I also think that your mates needed this information—as does our king."

Isabelle gasped. Why in the world would they have to bother the king with this ridiculous story? What did it matter now, anyway? It was all so long ago. And her father was dead. But her grandfather...

Realization dawned. Her family connections might somehow help the king. If so, she was honor-bound to use them. She knew what her answer would be even before the question came up. As far as she was concerned, she was Draconian. This country was the one that had taken her in and given her refuge. She was loyal to the country that had protected her and her mother for so very long.

"If you believe these claims that strongly, then yes, tell the king. I will do whatever he wishes," Isabelle said in a firm voice, finding her backbone now that her path was clear. "I have no emotional ties to those other lands, but if my existence as a loyal daughter of Draconia can help in some way, I am prepared to do whatever the king asks of me."

Everyone gathered around that table—dragon and human alike—seemed to release a collective breath of relief. Isabelle knew she had made the right decision. These people were her family, and this land was her home. She might be interested in meeting her grandfather if he could be convinced to have words with a mere human, but if he rejected her, then so be it. She had her mates now, and they were all she would ever need, from this day forward, to make her truly happy.

"You had all better start collecting your cold weather gear," Tilly sent in an amused, eager voice through their minds. *"It sounds like sooner or later, we're all going to be making a trip to the North."*

ABOUT THE AUTHOR

Bianca D'Arc has run a laboratory, climbed the corporate ladder in the shark-infested streets of lower Manhattan, studied and taught martial arts, and earned the right to put a whole bunch of letters after her name, but she's always enjoyed writing more than any of her other pursuits. She grew up and still lives on Long Island, where she keeps busy with an extensive garden, several aquariums full of very demanding fish, and writing her favorite genres of paranormal, fantasy and sci-fi romance.

Bianca loves to hear from readers and can be reached through Twitter (@BiancaDArc), Facebook (BiancaDArcAuthor) or through the various links on her website.

WELCOME TO THE D'ARC SIDE…
WWW.BIANCADARC.COM

OTHER BOOKS BY BIANCA D'ARC

Now Available

Brotherhood of Blood
One & Only
Rare Vintage
Phantom Desires
Sweeter Than Wine
Forever Valentine
Wolf Hills
Wolf Quest

Tales of the Were
Lords of the Were
Inferno

Tales of the Were – The Others
Rocky
Slade

Tales of the Were – Redstone Clan
Grif
Red
Magnus
Bobcat
Matt

String of Fate
Cat's Cradle
King's Throne
Jacob's Ladder
Her Warriors

Guardians of the Dark
Half Past Dead
Once Bitten, Twice Dead
A Darker Shade of Dead
The Beast Within
Dead Alert

Dragon Knights
Maiden Flight
The Dragon Healer
Border Lair
Master at Arms
The Ice Dragon
Prince of Spies
Wings of Change
FireDrake
Dragon Storm
Keeper of the Flame
Hidden Dragons

Resonance Mates
Hara's Legacy
Davin's Quest
Jaci's Experiment
Grady's Awakening
Harry's Sacrifice

Jit'Suku Chronicles
Arcana: King of Swords
Arcana: King of Cups
Arcana: King of Clubs
End of the Line

StarLords: Hidden Talent

Gifts of the Ancients
Warrior's Heart

Print Anthologies
Ladies of the Lair
I Dream of Dragons Vol. 1
Brotherhood of Blood
Caught by Cupid

String of Fate
KING'S THRONE

A woman living in secret, hiding her true nature...

Gina is a medical doctor in New York City. What nobody knows is that she's also tiger-shifter royalty, living in exile. Keeping her secret has kept her safe, but all that is about to change.

An injured soldier who heals in a way that makes him more than he ever was before...

Mitch is injured and out of the action. He wakes up in a strange place, with a beautiful woman. Normally, not a problem, but this woman is special. She's a white tiger and daughter of the lost tiger king. She's too good for the likes of him, but there's an undeniable spark of attraction drawing them closer and closer.

A love that will make the very earth tremble beneath their feet...

When evil challenges, Mitch will fight to keep Gina safe. A harrowing journey to the side of a living volcano brings secret knowledge and a power none of them ever expected. Will it be enough to prevail?

Only victory will keep his lady safe. And only victory will allow Gina to claim the man she truly loves.

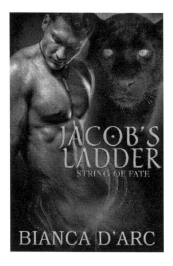

String of Fate
JACOB'S LADDER

A man on a mission...

Jake can see the future and there's a special woman on his mind. She needs his help and he's just the man to help when danger stalks her every step.

A woman with responsibilities...

For Ria, being the Nyx - the leader of her people - comes with burdens that few can understand. Her special abilities make her a target of the Venifucus, an ancient faction that hopes to pervert Ria's hereditary power to their own evil purposes. She's lived her life on the run, but the time has come to turn and confront the bad guys on her trail.

Can they stop the Venifucus from using the ancient power of the Nyx to return evil to this world? Whatever the cost, they must stop it, before it's too late.

String of Fate
HER WARRIORS

Love triangles are always more interesting when they come equipped with claws...and flippers?

Beau has anger issues, but not when he's around Jacki. The fierce tiger shifter has been following her around like a puppy, but she hasn't taken notice of him...until now.

No matter how long Geir has lived in the States, he's still the odd man out. A tiger shifter native of Iceland, he is a Master of his craft, training other warriors the skills he has perfected. When he sees Jacki for the first time, he knows she is the one for him.

Jacki is the privileged daughter of a prominent shifter Clan. Most of her relatives are lion shifters, so she knows how to handle cats on the prowl, but she is a much rarer selkie - a seal shifter - imbued with magic and surrounded by mystery. When an opportunity arises to step into a key role in shifter society, she is uncertain, but willing to try. And when she's told she doesn't have to choose between the two tigers, but rather, can have them both, she is more than intrigued. But someone is stalking their path and they must work together to nullify the danger, all while trying to figure out a complicated relationship that has all three of them questioning fate.

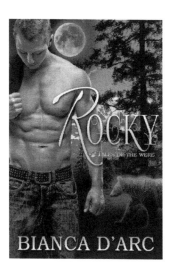

TALES OF THE WERE ~ THE OTHERS
ROCKY

On the run from her husband's killers, there is only one man who can help her now... her Rock.

Maggie is on the run from those who killed her husband nine months ago. She knows the only one who can help her is Rocco, a grizzly shifter she knew in her youth. She arrives on his doorstep in labor with twins. Magical, shapeshifting, bear cub twins destined to lead the next generation of werecreatures in North America.

Rocky is devastated by the news of his Clan brother's death, but he cannot deny the attraction that has never waned for the small human woman who stole his heart a long time ago. Rocky absented himself from her life when she chose to marry his childhood friend, but the years haven't changed the way he feels for her.

And now there are two young lives to protect. Rocky will do everything in his power to end the threat to the small family and claim them for himself. He knows he is the perfect Alpha to teach the cubs as they grow into their power... if their mother will let him love her as he has always longed to do.

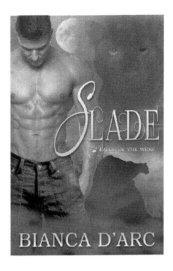

TALES OF THE WERE ~ THE OTHERS
SLADE

The fate of all shifters rests on his broad shoulders, but all he can think of is her.

Slade is a warrior and spy sent to Nevada to track a brutal murderer before the existence of all shifters is revealed to a world not ready to know.

Kate is a priestess serving the large community of shifters that have gathered around the Redstone cougars. When their matriarch is murdered and the scene polluted by dark magic, she knows she must help the enigmatic man sent to track the killer.

Together, Slade and Kate find not one but two evil mages that they alone can neutralize. Slade finds it hard to keep his hands off his sexy new partner, the cougars are out for blood, and the killers have an even more sinister plan in mind.

Can Kate somehow keep her hands to herself when the most attractive man she's ever met makes her want to throw caution to the wind? And can Slade do his job and save the situation when he's finally found a woman who can make him purr?

Warning: Contains a tiny bit of sexy ménage action with two smokin' hot men..

TALES OF THE WERE ~ REDSTONE CLAN 1
GRIF

Griffon Redstone is the eldest of five brothers and the leader of one of the most influential shifter Clans in North America. He seeks solace in the mountains, away from the horrific events of the past months, for both himself and his young sister. The deaths of their older sister and mother have hit them both very hard.

Lindsey Tate is human, but very aware of the werewolf Pack that lives near her grandfather's old cabin. She's come to right a wrong her grandfather committed against the Pack and salvage what's left of her family's honor—if the wolves will let her. Mostly, they seem intent on running her out of town on a rail.

But the golden haired stranger, Grif, comes to her rescue more than once. He stands up for her against the wolf Pack and then helps her fix the old generator at the cabin. When she performs a ceremony she expects will end in her death, the shifter deity has other ideas. Thrown together by fate, neither of them can deny their deep attraction, but will an old enemy tear them apart?

Warning: Frisky cats get up to all sorts of naughtiness, including a frenzy-induced multi-partner situation that might be a little intense for some readers.

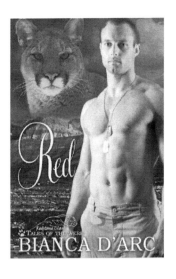

TALES OF THE WERE ~ REDSTONE CLAN 2
RED

A water nymph and a werecougar meet in a bar fight… No joke.

Steve Redstone agrees to keep an eye on his friend's little sister while she's partying in Las Vegas. He's happy to do the favor for an old Army buddy. What he doesn't expect is the wild woman who heats his blood and attracts too much attention from Others in the area.

Steve ends up defending her honor, breaking his cover and seducing the woman all within hours of meeting her, but he's helpless to resist her. She is his mate and that startling fact is going to open up a whole can of worms with her, her brother and the rest of the Redstone Clan.

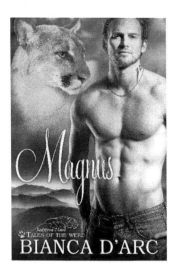

TALES OF THE WERE ~ REDSTONE CLAN 3
MAGNUS

A tortured vampire, a lonely shifter, and a deadly power struggle of supernatural proportions. Can their forbidden love prevail?

Magnus is the quiet brother. The one who keeps to himself. But he has good reason for his loner status. Two years ago, he met a woman. Not just any woman. This woman made his inner cougar stand up and roar. Even in human form, he purred when she stroked him, a sure sign that she was his mate. And mating is a very serious thing among shifters. Too bad the lady had fangs...

Mag discovers Miranda being held captive. She's been tortured to the point of -madness. Mag frees her and takes her to his home, nursing her back to health and defying all convention to keep her with him. He doesn't ever want to let her go again, but he knows the deck is stacked against them.

When a vampire uprising threatens, Mag and Miranda are in the middle. More than just their necks are on the line when a group of vampires seek to kill them and overthrow the current Master. But they have powerful allies, and their renewed relationship has made both of them stronger than either would ever be alone.

Can they stay together forever? Or will the daylight—and their two very different worlds—tear them apart again?

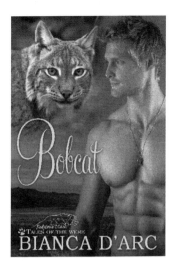

TALES OF THE WERE ~ REDSTONE CLAN
BOBCAT

On a mission far from home, he finds a sweet vulnerable lady...

Bob is a cougar shifter, one of the elite Redstone Alphas. On a mission for his Clan, he meets a fragile young woman, and finds himself drawn to her as never before.

A woman with a brutal past...

Serena is a bobcat shifter. Orphaned at the age of six, she was raised among humans until she was just barely a teen. Discovered by a Clan of unscrupulous bobcats, she was adopted and beaten on a regular basis because she refused to be a mule for their drug trade across the US-Canadian border. She doesn't have a lot of experience with men, but when she meets Bob Redstone, she finds him nearly irresistible.

A savage attack...

When their haven comes under siege, they take to the road. Bob has been tasked with keeping her safe, but they're also on a mission to find a mysterious warrior-shaman who's gone off the grid. Finding him means returning to Serena's former territory and possibly confronting those who abused her trust so badly, but they have no other choice.

Can she overcome her past to embrace the future with a man who could very well be her mate?

WWW.BIANCADARC.COM

20265648R00093

Made in the USA
San Bernardino, CA
03 April 2015